by

Lelia Eye

One Good Sonnet Publishing
Publishers of Fine Romance
and Fantasy Fiction

By Lelia Eye

Published by One Good Sonnet Publishing:

PRIDE AND PREJUDICE ADAPTATIONS

Netherfield's Secret

CO-AUTHORED WITH JANN ROWLAND

A Bevy of Suitors
A Summer in Brighton
Love and Laughter: A Pride and Prejudice Short Stories Anthology
Waiting for an Echo, Volume One: Words in the Darkness
Waiting for an Echo, Volume Two: Echoes at Dawn

CO-AUTHORED WITH JANN ROWLAND AND COLIN ROWLAND

Mistletoe and Mischief: A Pride and Prejudice Christmas Anthology

FAIRYTALES/FANTASY

The Princes and the Peas
The Smothered Rose Trilogy, Book One: Thorny
The Smothered Rose Trilogy, Book Two: Unsoiled
The Smothered Rose Trilogy, Book Three: Roseblood

CO-AUTHORED WITH JANN ROWLAND

The Earth and Sky Trilogy, Book One: On Wings of Air
The Earth and Sky Trilogy, Book Two: Lonely Paths
*The Earth and Sky Trilogy, Book Three: On Tides of Fate**

*Forthcoming

This is a work of fiction based on the works of Jane Austen. All the characters and events portrayed in this novel are products of Jane Austen's original novel or the author's imagination or are used fictitiously.

A SISTER'S SACRIFICE

Published by One Good Sonnet Publishing

ISBN: 1989212360
ISBN-13: 9781989212363

This is dedicated to everyone who is willing to sacrifice something for the well-being of their family members.

ACKNOWLEDGMENTS

Many thanks to my husband and my two children.

Many thanks as well to Jann Rowland for his continual assistance and support.

CHAPTER I

For the industrious, the lively, the playful, a brisk walk can serve to infuse the body with energy and clear the mind of extraneous thoughts. For Elizabeth Bennet, her morning constitutional was almost sacred due to its immediate and lasting benefits, even now, as winter assailed her senses with its chilly breezes and frostbitten foliage.

Elizabeth loved the sensation of crisp, fresh air on her face as her feet carried her forward into the ever-changing scenery of the natural world. Rare was the occasion when she felt anything less than revived by her foray into the outdoors.

On this particular day, however, as she began to return to Longbourn from her morning stroll, no feelings of rebirth or refreshment settled upon her; rather, she found her heart troubled and her thoughts ponderous.

"Why has my dear sister not sent it?" wondered Elizabeth. "Could she have forgotten what we discussed?"

Elizabeth had been waiting for a month and a half to receive a specific sort of letter from her dearest sister, but the correspondence that had reached her hands was scant, brief, and utterly unlike that which she had been desirous of seeing.

Jane, who was the eldest of the five Bennet sisters, was staying at a London townhouse owned by her fiancé's aunt. She had been taken under said aunt's wing with all the eagerness of a mother hen (and—if one were to imagine the great woman's vocalization of the imperious-sounding letter she had sent—all the obstreperousness of a territorial cock). But whereas the aunt's few letters to the family reporting on Jane's progress were lengthy and condescending, Jane's letters were curt and reserved. In short, they were nothing like the young woman herself.

To call Elizabeth disconcerted by this development was to put it mildly. Never had she expected to characterize the sister dearest to her heart in anything less than glowing terms. She scarcely dared to speculate on what could have caused Jane to act in such an atypical fashion. Before leaving for London, Jane had indicated she would, as had been suggested by her fiancé's aunt, invite Elizabeth to join her after she had become more acclimated to her new place on the London scene. However, no such invitation had ever arrived. Rather, it seemed as if Jane wished to warn Elizabeth to stay away, though those words were never actually put to paper.

"Until I see the extent of Jane's situation, I shall not be convinced that her fiancé's family is treating her well," thought Elizabeth to herself.

If her sister were indeed the target of some social villainy, Elizabeth would do anything within her power to extract Jane from her engagement, no matter what consequences arose from her intervention.

Her determination blazing to life, Elizabeth settled on a scheme to elicit an invitation to London from her aunt. With ever-growing eagerness, she hastened her steps toward Longbourn.

When Mrs. Gardiner's return letter finally arrived a few days later, Elizabeth sequestered herself in her room. Living in a house that included three other sisters and a mother prone to complaining meant that solitude was in short supply. As such, reading a letter in the drawing-room with her sisters and mother nearby could not be accomplished without drawing excessive curiosity and shrill noise, neither of which was particularly welcome. Only Mr. Bennet would show any disinterest—at least, such would be the case until he noticed what effect a particularly interesting piece of correspondence had on her.

After unfolding the letter, Elizabeth began to read it:

"MY DEAREST LIZZY,

"I shall own that the arrival of your letter came at a most fortuitous time, for the sentiments it expressed were not unlike those which have been troubling my heart for some time. I have been contemplating inviting you to come to London, yet I had hesitated to do so because I did not want to cause you undue concern. I suppose I should have known better, as you have always been so finely attuned to Jane that even a great distance cannot obscure the fact that something is amiss. I wish I could say that I would be glad to have you join me and my family at our home, but the truth is that the circumstances under which you will be commencing your journey are none which I would ever wish upon you.

"During Jane's time in London, I have only seen her twice. Certainly, I had expected to see her much more often than has been the case. Perhaps part of the reason for our dearth of time together can be attributed to her fiancé's aunt, who I understand to be a rather officious and matronly sort, but the situation cannot be so easily dismissed, for your sister seems to have lost some of her warmth and her willingness to confide in me. She will now not speak even one word where unnecessary, and I should sooner guess at the emotional state of a clam than Jane's feelings now.

"Perhaps it may all be attributed to the fact that her company is different and unfamiliar. I rather think you should encourage your sisters to come to town with you. Perhaps the sight of well-known faces can melt the ice that appears to have taken residence in our dear Jane's eyes."

Though she had not yet finished reading the letter, Elizabeth set it aside for a moment. If such great concern had beset Mrs. Gardiner, then Elizabeth's worries and fears could only be deemed confirmed. Something had dampened Jane's spirits—Elizabeth only hoped they were merely dampened and not crushed—and it fell upon Elizabeth to determine the cause.

When the family gathered for dinner, Elizabeth advised that Mrs. Gardiner had issued an invitation to her home in London.

"Congratulations, Lizzy," said Mr. Bennet with an expression that was more of a smirk than a smile. "Provided the weather continues to permit travel, it appears you have been given the opportunity to escape the silliness of Longbourn and spend time with people of sense."

"I do not believe Lizzy needs to travel to London simply to escape the company of her family," said Mary, the third-born of the Bennet sisters. "Certainly, the society of London is not to my liking, but I am able to find refuge in the wisdom of Fordyce while at home, for I am, as you know, of a serious mind that has no need for such amusements as can be found in London. However, I do believe Jane would be comforted to have one of her sisters close at hand."

The youngest Bennet, Lydia, never had any patience for Mary, but she moved past her annoyance to proclaim: "Kitty and I have no desire to leave the company of redcoats who have come to the area. La! The fact that you should consider doing so is very odd, Lizzy!"

"I think your sisters have the right of it, Lizzy," said Mrs. Bennet. "I should not mind having a daughter or two married to a military gentleman. Perhaps it would be better if you attempted to procure a husband from the solicitous redcoats with whom we have been blessed, for the gentlemen in London may not wish to take any notice of you at all."

"I am afraid I must disagree with you, my dear," said Mr. Bennet. "I believe it more likely that Elizabeth should find a worthy gentleman in London. As I am more inclined to think that the color of a man's coat does not in any way reflect the quality of his character, I believe that if my Lizzy has not yet had her head turned by any men in the militia, she might be better served setting her cap at someone new."

"Mr. Bennet," said his wife, "you know that a husband may not be selected and won in a day or even a week—"

"On the contrary, my dear," said Mr. Bennet, "I had rather thought that falling in and out of love was a quick undertaking, much like when Lydia is involved in selecting bonnets. Choosing a suitor must be simple; it is determining whether the fit is proper that is a much more onerous process."

"I have no desire to hunt for men or bonnets while in town," said Elizabeth, who at present had little patience for any quibbling between her parents. "Instead, I should much prefer to be allowed the opportunity to speak with Jane about her circumstances in London. I doubt she has had occasion to befriend many other young women, and the difference in age between her and her fiancé's aunt is not likely to add to her comfort."

Elizabeth did not believe it would be worth further expounding upon her worries for fear that her father might tease her. However, she knew her concerns were genuine and reasonable. After all, she had not even met Jane's fiancé yet. He could very well be an inappropriate match for Jane despite his vaunted lineage. The only way she might have her fears alleviated would be to meet the young gentleman himself—assuming, of course, he demonstrated evidence of good breeding at such a meeting.

If he did not, then perhaps the engagement could be dissolved. For whatever reason, Mr. Bennet had wanted the engagement to be kept a secret from the public. As a result, only the couple's family members and close friends knew of the arrangement.

The secrecy of the prospective union was part of the reason for Elizabeth's anxiety. Mr. Bennet's and Jane's refusal to enlighten her on exactly how the engagement had been brought about did nothing to alleviate her concerns.

"Jane is comfortable in any company," said Mrs. Bennet dismissively. "You need not worry about her comportment."

Jane's comportment was the least of Elizabeth's worries, but she chose to ignore her mother's comment in favor of saying: "My dear aunt has also extended an invitation to my sisters. As they are not otherwise engaged, I believe they should come."

"Not otherwise engaged?" cried Lydia. "Why, Mrs. Forster and I have made all manner of plans to ensure any parties attended by the redcoats shall never be forgotten, for she and I are such good friends! We have even decided to dress Chamberlayne in women's clothes tomorrow to play a good joke on Colonel Forster's men. Of course, you must not tell a soul about our plans, for it would ruin all the fun!"

"Though I have no desire to participate in such frivolities as Lydia, believing that a young woman's time should be spent on the betterment of herself," said Mary with a disapproving look at Lydia, "I do not want to travel to London either. While I should not wish to depreciate the desire of others to experience the entertainments of London, I have been working on some important extracts that require my continued attention, and there are a few pieces that I am trying to perfect on the pianoforte. Travel to London should only hinder my progress."

In other circumstances, Elizabeth might have felt pleased by Lydia's and Mary's reluctance to accompany her to London simply because she did not wish to share the company of her favorite aunt with her sisters. However, Elizabeth had been worried about the occasional outrageousness of the behavior demonstrated by Kitty and Lydia upon the arrival of the regiment of militia, and as such, she appealed to her father's good sense:

"Papa, do you not think London society would be beneficial for my sisters? I fear too much time spent in the presence of militiamen might not be conducive to proper behavior—"

"Oh, Lizzy, you need not worry about your sisters' behavior," said Mrs. Bennet. "There is no harm in letting them have a piece of fun here and there. In fact, I should not be surprised if my dear Lydia obtains a fine husband among the officers. I have no doubt she would be much better served staying in Hertfordshire."

"Lizzy," said Mr. Bennet, "I am afraid that if I force Lydia to go, the sheer number of letters she will write in protest shall deplete the entire contents of my pocket-book."

With an aggrieved air, Elizabeth turned to Kitty. "Will you accompany me, Kitty?"

The young woman's face twisted, evidence that the idea did not particularly appeal to her, but to Elizabeth's surprise, she said: "I suppose I should not mind a trip to London."

A smile broke over Elizabeth's face. "You will not regret it, Kitty. I am certain my dear aunt will keep us well-entertained in town. You are older than you were the last time we were in London, and I should think more opportunities will have opened up for you."

Kitty's weak smile betrayed her lack of enthusiasm, but she merely nodded.

Elizabeth had to suppress a sigh of relief. While Lydia was a hopeless cause, Elizabeth might be able to curb some of Kitty's silliness in London. Though Kitty was a year older than Lydia, she tended to follow Lydia's schemes without question. Perhaps separating the two would lead to progress in both of their temperaments.

Still, at present, their behavior was the least of Elizabeth's concerns. For now, her primary focus was on Jane.

CHAPTER II

Once permission had been given for the trip to London, Elizabeth's eagerness to leave Longbourn seemed to grow in intensity. Of course, she could not depart immediately after receiving her dear aunt's letter, even had her trunks already been prepared. Since a manservant could not be spared, it was determined that Elizabeth and Kitty would leave in the company of a maid, though their mother complained loudly about the temporary loss, and there were other preparations to be made besides.

Once the morning on which they were to leave did arrive, the two young women took time to bid their family farewell in front of the carriage.

They first embraced their mother, who could not seem to determine whether she wished them to stay or go, and then they embraced Mary and Lydia. Mary had some fragment of a lecture on the importance of morality to pass on to them, which both young women ignored, and Lydia had a request for bonnet-trimmings that she repeated to Kitty, who acknowledged the request with unconcealed impatience.

Elizabeth and Kitty then looked to their father, who had been standing back. He limped forward, and Elizabeth masked her concern while she watched him. As her father grew older, his limp grew more pronounced, and though he would deny it if asked, Elizabeth suspected that his leg hurt him. Elizabeth and her sisters had asked him numerous times as to the origin of his limp and the scar on his face, but despite his usual interest in unveiling mysteries, he would always merely declare that it was a sacrifice he had been more than willing to make for his family. Kitty and Lydia had speculated that the limp was an old wound caused by a dramatic duel, but Elizabeth had not agreed with the notion that their father would have been so foolhardy.

"Tell your aunt she may not keep you too long, Lizzy," said Mr. Bennet. "Your absence compounded with Jane's means that it shall be quite some time before any intelligent conversation shall be found within the walls of Longbourn. Mayhap I should read some of my books aloud so that I can fill the empty air with substance."

"I will write to you, my dear father," said Elizabeth, "and then you may read my letters aloud to my mother and my sisters. Surely that shall sustain you until such time that I return."

"That is assuming you do not find a husband in London," said Mr. Bennet with the sigh of a suffering man.

"Regardless of whom I find in London, you need not worry that I will not return. Rather, pray that I shall find Jane well and that I shall not lose my penknife."

"Now, Lizzy, you need not give your father such a fright as that. If you fail to write to me, then I should almost certainly go mad."

Elizabeth embraced her father, assuring him that she would not neglect the task of writing to him. "Furthermore, I shall not even request that you undergo the onerous task of writing to me, for I know it is an effort you dare not undertake."

"Lizzy, I shall feel the effect of your absence so strongly that I would almost endeavor to write to you. However, you are aware that I am not nearly so diligent in keeping up with my own penknife. It must be the failure of my memory, you know, a sad result of my advanced age."

Though Elizabeth knew it was nothing of the sort, she could only give her dear father a smile.

The farewells were drawn out a little longer, but at last Elizabeth and Kitty set out in the carriage with the maid. Kitty seemed withdrawn in the absence of Lydia's company, but Elizabeth endeavored to draw her into conversation, and they had a pleasant enough journey.

When they arrived at Gracechurch Street, Elizabeth saw Mrs. Gardiner sitting near the drawing-room window, where she awaited their arrival. Once Mrs. Gardiner espied them, she hurried to meet them, her children following behind her. The children seemed eager to see their cousins, though they demonstrated a sudden shyness when it was time to actually speak.

However, when Kitty moved forward and began exclaiming over how much they had grown, the children were more inclined to converse, and soon it was difficult to make out their words, as they were all clamoring to be heard.

While Kitty tended to the children, Mrs. Gardiner and Elizabeth secluded themselves in a corner of the drawing-room.

"Mr. Gardiner is handling business matters," said Mrs. Gardiner, "but I know you have not come for the purpose of seeing him. You wish to hear more of Jane, I am sure."

"Please tell me anything that you know," said Elizabeth. "I am desperate for the barest scrap of information."

"I fear I do not have much to tell. As I wrote in my letter, I have only seen your sister twice since she came to London. I am still unaware as to whether she has been too occupied to see me or whether there is another reason. I hoped that you might be able to succeed in determining what has so affected her."

"You mentioned that you thought the changes might be attributed to her fiancé's aunt. Is there more to say on that subject?"

"As far as I can determine, the woman treats Jane well enough, but she appears to be a rather meddlesome sort. She lost her daughter some years back, and from what I have heard, she takes pleasure in escaping to London to take young women under her wing. This precedent has enabled the secrecy of your sister's engagement to be maintained, but I am not certain how long it shall last."

"The fact that it is necessary at all to keep the engagement from the public worries me, but my father has been unwilling to divulge the reason for such intrigue. I have wondered whether it is merely due to his fondness for the enigmatic."

"I do not think your father would insist upon such a thing for a paltry reason like that," said Mrs. Gardiner, "but if he is not inclined to explain himself, then I doubt you shall obtain the intelligence elsewhere."

"Jane has not been forthcoming, so I suspect you are correct. I suppose the truth shall be revealed when everyone involved decides it is time."

"Indeed."

The next day, Elizabeth, Kitty, and Mrs. Gardiner wasted no time in calling on Jane. Despite Mrs. Gardiner's warnings, Elizabeth found herself unprepared for the new personage before them.

Lady Catherine de Bourgh was a stern-faced and domineering sort of woman who obviously wished to exert control over everyone and everything around her. Even the furniture of her townhouse reflected her character, for it was not warm, comfortable, and inviting, but rather austere, large, and expensive. The only exception was a quaint old long-case clock that stood against the wall, its pendulum swinging back and forth as it quietly ticked away the time.

After the initial shock of Lady Catherine's overbearing presence had passed, Elizabeth focused much of her attention on Jane.

When Lady Catherine gave her the occasion to speak, Jane remained polite but distant. Jane did not appear to be cowed by her ladyship in the way that Kitty was, but she nonetheless seemed uninclined to bestow more than the barest minimum of courtesy on her family. Considering Elizabeth had always been apt to speak of Jane's kind nature in glowing terms, this development came as a surprise. She might have felt she had cause to be offended were it not for the pallor of Jane's features and the thinner nature of her face. While Jane did not appear to be ill, neither did she seem well.

"I understand from Miss Bennet that all five Bennet daughters are out," said Lady Catherine, oblivious to the gravity of Elizabeth's thoughts.

Suspecting Lady Catherine meant to rant about the impropriety of such a thing, Elizabeth replied firmly: "Indeed, we are. It would not be fair to allow the older daughters the opportunity to engage in society's entertainments while the younger daughters stay home."

Lady Catherine huffed in obvious disagreement but did not pursue the matter further. Instead, she glanced at Jane with a smile that, oddly enough, seemed almost fond. "I suppose you must wish to hear about the progress I have made with your older sister."

"We certainly appreciate all the assistance you have been providing her," said Mrs. Gardiner politely.

Elizabeth only frowned. Could the cause of Jane's weakened appearance be attributed to Lady Catherine's overbearing nature?

"As the scion of an earl, my nephew deserves only the best of brides, which was why I decided to bestow this particular favor upon someone who ordinarily would not draw my notice," said Lady

Catherine. "In pursuit of my goal of the improvement of Miss Bennet, I have made certain to introduce her to all manner of well-connected people, the better to assist her when she must move out in society on her own. I have also spent time improving her etiquette, and I have no doubt that she will do credit to the Darcy family name once the engagement is finally announced."

Elizabeth gritted her teeth in an effort not to gainsay her ladyship. As the epitome of grace and decorum, Jane had no need for assistance with etiquette. While meeting the upper-class sorts of people with whom the Darcys would associate could do naught but aid Jane, nobody could say anything ill of her manners.

Lady Catherine continued: "I believe my efforts may only be lauded at this point, for we have already made great strides."

"Yes, your ladyship," said Jane quietly in agreement.

Elizabeth looked at her sister, wishing to find some hint of emotion there, but whatever Jane felt could not be read on her face.

"As the mistress of Rosings Park," said Lady Catherine, "I have served as a hostess countless times, and I soon intend to host an intimate meal wherein I shall teach your sister everything she needs to know concerning how to act as a proper hostess."

"We have had occasion to have guests at Longbourn," began Elizabeth.

Lady Catherine sniffed at the notion. "A country meal is nothing compared to the sort of meal that is to be found in London—even an intimate meal among family and close friends such as the one I am planning."

Elizabeth did not miss the warning look given to her by Mrs. Gardiner. Knowing she should not try to aggravate Lady Catherine, Elizabeth looked to Jane. "Have you had occasion to speak much with your fiancé, Jane?"

Her ladyship spoke before Jane could. "You need not worry about your sister. Young Darcy is a charming sort of fellow, though I had always believed that my late sister, his mother, Lady Anne, should have put more effort into reining him in. I had rather hoped that he would be destined for a wealthy and prestigious match, but I suppose there is no help for it now. To make up for any deficiencies, I will ensure that Miss Bennet becomes a wife in whom he may take pride."

Elizabeth had attempted to temper her anger, but she could only withstand so much of Lady Catherine's disparagement of Jane. "Your ladyship—"

"I have learned much from Lady Catherine," said Jane, "and I am very appreciative of her efforts to assist me in navigating the hidden dangers of London society."

Elizabeth looked at her sister, who rarely interrupted anyone. Perhaps the fact that she had attempted to save Elizabeth from castigating Lady Catherine served as evidence that the old Jane remained buried beneath this cold façade.

"Jane, I wonder whether you might take a turn about the room with me," said Elizabeth, desiring to pull her sister away briefly for a private conversation.

"I should prefer to remain where I am, if you do not mind," said Jane softly, refusing to meet Elizabeth's eyes. "I fear I am a little fatigued."

"It would be much too difficult for us to carry on our conversation with the two of you circling the drawing-room like birds," said Lady Catherine. "I believe it would be far better if you stretched your legs after you depart, Miss Elizabeth."

Though disappointed that she could not partake in more intimate conversation with her sister, Elizabeth merely indicated her acknowledgment of her ladyship's words.

"Now," said Lady Catherine, "a good acquaintance of mine is hosting a private ball in two days' time to which I mean to escort Miss Bennet. It should not be any hardship for me to obtain an invitation directed toward her sisters, and I believe she might find herself to be more comfortable with family present. I expect my youngest nephew to be there. As I understand it, you have not yet met your sister's fiancé."

After eagerly indicating her agreement to attend the ball, Elizabeth glanced at Kitty and added: "I believe it would be a good opportunity for Kitty to expand her society."

Kitty looked at Elizabeth with a slightly raised brow. Elizabeth merely gave her a mere shake of the head. Expanding Kitty's society had nothing to do with Elizabeth's eagerness. Instead, the primary thought on Elizabeth's mind was her desire to see what sort of man Jane would be marrying.

Chapter III

The day of the ball referenced by Lady Catherine dawned, and the morning hours seemed to melt away with the aggravating slowness of dripping molasses. Elizabeth had been waiting for some time to meet Jane's fiancé, and now the meeting was close at hand, she felt she could scarcely wait another minute.

Finally, however, Mr. and Mrs. Gardiner agreed it was time to depart Gracechurch Street, and they escorted their two impatient nieces outside with knowing smiles.

After arriving at their destination, they soon found that the ballroom was already crowded. Despite the large numbers of people, Kitty quickly found Jane and pointed her out to Elizabeth. Though surprised at the ease with which Kitty espied Jane, Elizabeth supposed it could be attributed to Lady Catherine, whom Jane stood beside. Her ladyship was a proud island in a chaotic sea, standing tall despite her age, her eyes sharp as flint while she surveyed her surroundings, and her mouth grim whenever she found people nearby wanting. In contrast, Jane was a thin tree clinging to said island, handsome as ever but with a spirit that seemed to bow underneath the strength of any winds that assailed her. Elizabeth felt as if her own heart broke a little whenever she looked upon her.

As they approached her ladyship, Elizabeth heard the woman detailing the importance of various personages in the ballroom:

"—And Mr. Covington, though he is descended from an earl, is hardly to be respected due to some questionable choices made in his youth. However, his sister, Mrs. Andrews, is the sort of woman whom you would do well to befriend. Her connections are wide and varying, yet of particular note is the fact that she is close friends with a duchess."

Lady Catherine continued to prattle on for a few minutes, not having noticed the arrival of the Gardiners and their charges, but Jane witnessed her family's approach quickly. Her expression became almost pained at the sight, but whenever Lady Catherine paused in the midst of her ramble, Jane ventured to greet the Gardiners and her two sisters quietly.

Having now caught sight of the newcomers, Lady Catherine offered her own perfunctory greeting, and then she said: "I have been educating Miss Bennet on the notable persons in whose company she is liable to be in London. Miss Elizabeth and Miss Catherine, though your society shall not be the same as Miss Bennet's, I suspect it might behoove both of you to take note of what I have to say. After all, good breeding could draw the eye of an unfamiliar gentleman this evening, and the Master of Ceremonies might seek to facilitate an introduction, so knowledge will be of the utmost importance as you determine how to proceed."

"If it is as her ladyship says," said Elizabeth, "and Kitty and I will not move among the same society as Jane, then I believe our time would be better spent learning more about the acquaintances we are making rather than learning about strangers we may never have occasion to meet."

Lady Catherine stared at Elizabeth for a long moment before replying. "You have decided opinions for one so young."

"Opinions belong to everyone, your ladyship. Wonder should not be enkindled by the possession of opinions, but rather by the method of expressing them."

Lady Catherine, judging by her countenance, appeared to be unable to determine whether to be offended or impressed by Elizabeth's response.

"Your manner is dissimilar to that of your sister's," said Lady Catherine suddenly.

"Certainly, I do not aspire to be an angel like Jane," said Elizabeth with a smile. "I should find more interest in making light of a person's foibles than explaining them away as Jane would."

Lady Catherine made a noise that could have been acknowledgment or agreement, and then she beheld someone else whom she knew, which led to her proffering yet another detailed explanation of the social intricacies involving the ballroom's inhabitants.

A few minutes later, a young woman and a gentleman walked up to their party and interrupted Lady Catherine's expostulation. Though slightly haughty in demeanor, the young woman appeared to be glad to see Jane. Introductions were made, and Elizabeth learned that the gentleman was Edward Livingston and the lady was his wife, Caroline Livingston.

"They are newly married," said Lady Catherine, dispensing her knowledge with all the condescension that was her wont. "Mrs. Livingston is the sister of Charles Bingley, who is the particular friend of one of my nephews."

After courtesies were exchanged between Elizabeth's family and the couple, Mrs. Livingston turned her attention to Jane. "Ah, my dear Jane! I have missed you these past few days. I fear I have been kept away by my husband, who seems entirely too keen on making me attend to his friends rather than my own."

Jane murmured some reply in response, but Elizabeth was not close enough to hear what it was. Then Mrs. Livingston leaned forward and whispered something to Jane which Elizabeth again could not make out.

"I understand you come from a large family in Hertfordshire," said Mr. Livingston to Elizabeth and Kitty.

"We do indeed," said Elizabeth. "Two of my younger sisters remained at home while Kitty and I came to town."

"I hail from a family of six children."

"Do you indeed?" asked Elizabeth distantly, glancing at Jane and Mrs. Livingston, wishing she were close enough to understand their conversation.

"I do."

Elizabeth waited for a moment for Mr. Livingston to say more, but when he did not, she began to suspect that the man was not precisely in possession of a great intellect. "Are you the eldest?"

"I am."

Elizabeth looked at Kitty, at a loss as to how to continue speaking to such a poor conversationalist.

Kitty apparently received the call for help, as she stepped in. "I do not believe I caught the name of your estate, Mr. Livingston."

"Linfield Manor," said he.

"Are you fond of your home?"

"I am."

"I am given to understand that Linfield Manor is an estate of more than moderate prominence," said Mr. Gardiner, who had been attending to the conversation.

Mr. Livingston gave a wide smile. "It does well, but I have become even fonder of it since it received a mistress."

Though Elizabeth had grown increasingly frustrated by his inability to properly maintain a conversation, she softened at the obvious love and pride in his eyes. Even if he were not London's greatest intellect, he did seem to love his wife.

Before anyone could respond, he straightened his back eagerly and said: "Ah, Langley! I apologize, but you must please excuse me, for I see a friend with whom I need to speak."

Then, after bows and curtsies were exchanged, Mr. Livingston tendered a loving smile to his wife and excused himself.

Kitty, who appeared to have been surveying the room, told Elizabeth: "I hope I do not have to sit out many dances. At home, the redcoats would keep me busy the whole evening."

"More important than the number of dances is the quality of your partners," said Elizabeth in gentle admonishment. "You need not worry about missing the redcoats and their frivolities. In London, you should concentrate on making more meaningful connections."

The appearance of three gentlemen and a subsequent flurry of introductions interrupted Elizabeth's well-meaning lecture, and while she might ordinarily have been annoyed at having a lesson diverted, one of the gentlemen was someone whom she had been quite desirous of meeting.

When the gentlemen were introduced, she gave Fitzwilliam Darcy, a tall and dark-haired man with a somber countenance and a handsome face, only a cursory look. Charles Bingley, a good-looking young man with a pleasant smile and bright eyes, also received only a moment of notice. At that time, she found her attention primarily focused on Henry Darcy. He was, after all, Jane's fiancé.

"Mr. Bingley is staying at my nephew Darcy's townhouse, as is Henry," said Lady Catherine. Privately, Elizabeth could not blame

Mr. Bingley for having decided not to stay with the Livingstons. "Henry does not yet have a house in town, though I have tried to encourage him to consider the prospect."

"Why should I maintain a house in town when my brother can take on all the cost and I can reap all the benefit?" asked Mr. Henry Darcy dryly. But though he had spoken to his aunt, he seemed to be focusing little of his attention on her.

Indeed, though the young man had come upon his fiancée for the first time that evening, he seemed to hold no more interest in speaking to her than to a stranger; in fact, *more* of his attention was given to Elizabeth and Kitty and the Gardiners, for he did not even glance at Jane.

He was handsome enough, Elizabeth supposed, with dark features not unlike his brother's and a roguish look about him. He appeared to be about the same height as Mr. Darcy—perhaps a little shorter—and Elizabeth wanted to like him for Jane's sake. However, she could not help but feel less than impressed, as if she had been expecting a swan but only found a common drake.

"It is a pleasure to meet Miss Bennet's sisters," said Mr. Henry Darcy with a smile that bordered on a leer as he gazed upon Elizabeth and Kitty. "I had not realized you would be so handsome."

"We have two more sisters at home," said Elizabeth, trying not to let her discomfort show. The others of their group appeared to have had their attention captured by Lady Catherine, whose vociferousness was wince-inducing. "Jane is the handsomest of us all."

"Your color is somewhat darker," said he, "but certainly no less pleasing."

Made even more uncomfortable by his undisguised scrutiny, Elizabeth said: "I am afraid I must disagree with you, for Jane is considered to be the jewel of Hertfordshire."

Mr. Henry Darcy made a noncommittal noise, and his gaze moved from her to traverse the room, as if her continual compliments of his fiancée bored him.

"I should think you might be more aware than anyone of her charms," murmured Elizabeth, speaking for his ears only as she tried to test his commitment to her sister.

"And what of *your* charms, Miss Elizabeth?" asked he, speaking at a comfortable volume and ignoring her implication. "Have you come to London to experience its . . . entertainments?"

Irritated by this young gentleman and his prevarications, Elizabeth glanced at Jane. To one who did not know her, Jane had all the appearance of someone who was listening to Lady Catherine's proclamations. But Elizabeth could tell from the way Jane so determinedly avoided meeting her eyes that Jane was actually focused on Henry's words.

"I have come to London to see Jane," replied Elizabeth firmly.

Henry Darcy seemed to be too distracted to reply, intent as he was upon admiring the forms of two young women walking by.

After biting back the caustic words with which she wished to flay the young man, Elizabeth began to attend to the speech of Lady Catherine.

"I suppose it is now time for the young men to collect their dances," said her ladyship. "I believe the young women should be free at present." She then looked over at her younger nephew. "Henry."

Distracted, the young man did not even look at her when he replied. "Yes, your ladyship?"

"Miss Bennet has not yet been engaged for any dances."

Lady Catherine's statement seeped into the young man's awareness, and he glanced at her and then, for the first time since Elizabeth had made his acquaintance, looked at Jane.

"Miss Bennet," said he coolly, "will you save a set for me?"

There was nothing of love or admiration in his gaze, nothing of interest or even respect. Instead, the distance between him and his betrothed might as well have been an entire ocean as a few feet, for all the concern Henry Darcy held for Jane.

Jane, for her part, did not seem to be affected by Mr. Henry Darcy either. She confirmed that she would dance with him, and once a set had been selected, she and the gentleman each ceased to acknowledge the existence of the other. Mr. Henry Darcy obviously considered his duty to be done, and he once more diverted his attention from his party to the crowd of people milling around him. He showed no inclination to collect a set from Elizabeth or Kitty.

By this point, Elizabeth believed she had taken her measure of him, and she remained heartily disappointed. Perhaps the reason for such distance between Jane and him was because they had recently argued—

"No," thought Elizabeth firmly. The notion of Jane arguing with any young man in such a fashion as to anger him was ridiculous. Rather, the young man concerned himself with the looks of women rather than their substance, and he could be swayed more by a pretty face than a selfless heart.

Even disregarding the present circumstances, Elizabeth found it impossible to deny that Henry Darcy was lacking. After all, he had not seen fit to visit the Bennets at Longbourn and meet Jane's sisters. He had come once or twice to speak with Mr. Bennet, but he had never deigned to even seek an introduction to the other members of the family. Perhaps his poor manners were the reason for the engagement's secrecy.

Fortunately, Mr. Bingley at least endeavored to extend the common courtesies expected, eagerly requesting a dance from the three Bennets. Kitty seemed particularly cheered by the prospect of having a dance lined up, which in turn caused Elizabeth to feel a certain burgeoning fondness for Mr. Bingley.

Smiling, Elizabeth glanced from Mr. Bingley to the Darcys. She could see Mr. Darcy murmuring something to his brother, who rolled his eyes. Mr. Darcy said something sharply in response, and Henry Darcy gave a begrudging nod.

"Miss Elizabeth," said the young man with an unnecessary flourish that must have been for his brother's benefit, "would you honor me with a dance?"

Though tempted to deal a blow to the man's vanity by declining, Elizabeth did not do so, as it would mean she would have to forego dancing with Mr. Bingley. That gentleman, at least, was pleasant and worthy of gracing with smiles.

After Elizabeth agreed to dance with Mr. Henry Darcy, there was a pause in which she half-expected him to request a set from Kitty as well. When he did not, Elizabeth glanced at her younger sister, who had an unmistakable look of disappointment written on her face.

Offended on Kitty's behalf, Elizabeth looked at Mr. Henry Darcy, whose attention had once more been withdrawn from his present company, and then at Mr. Darcy, whose perturbation was evident in the tightness of his mouth. No doubt he had advised his brother that it would only be proper to request dances from both Elizabeth and Kitty.

Mr. Darcy rallied quickly, however, and he requested dances from the three Bennets and Mrs. Livingston. Jane remained unreadable, Mrs. Livingston preened as if it were only her due, and Kitty gave a wide smile to Mr. Darcy in appreciation. Though she had been stricken before by Mr. Henry Darcy's neglect, now Kitty seemed happy indeed.

Mrs. Livingston murmured something to Jane, and the other young woman's response was inaudible. Elizabeth frowned at the sight, wondering whether the relationship between Jane and

Mrs. Livingston should be discouraged or whether the reason for her own discomfort could be something as simple as envy.

"Mrs. Gardiner," said Mr. Bingley, "I wonder whether you might deign to grace me with a dance as well. I should be honored were you to do so."

Mrs. Gardiner laughed. "I held more interest in the card tables than the dance floor when I came here tonight, Mr. Bingley."

"Surely you will be able to enjoy a dance or two while still satisfying your obligations at cards," said Mr. Bingley warmly.

"Certainly, you are correct, Mr. Bingley. I will gladly dance a set with you. I suppose I had intended to dance with my husband regardless."

Though still expressionless, Jane looked between Mr. Bingley and her aunt. Before Jane had left for London, Elizabeth had thought herself aware of the entirety of her eldest sister's thoughts; now, however, she could not have ventured even the merest guess.

When Elizabeth noticed Mr. Bingley studying Jane, she wondered at it. Could he have some concerns about her sister as well? If so, what could it mean? His lips were pursed in thought, and the slight furrow of his brow only further indicated his preoccupation.

When he noticed Elizabeth's gaze, he broke into a smile and flushed, looking away.

"Mr. Darcy," said Mrs. Livingston suddenly, "is your sister well? It has been far too long since I have seen dear Georgiana. Is she still playing the pianoforte?"

A fond expression came over Mr. Darcy's face. "She practices the pianoforte regularly and is doing well, thank you."

"Has she grown since I last saw her?"

"I suspect she has."

Their conversation continued in this fashion for a few minutes, with Mr. Darcy proving himself taciturn, but not rude. Still, even the limited discourse between him and Mrs. Livingston impressed Elizabeth far more than what she had witnessed from Mr. Henry Darcy. As for Charles Bingley, he was the most impressive of all. It would have been far better if *he* had been the one who decided to pay court to Jane.

The situation vexed her. If Henry Darcy had proven himself to be attentive to Jane, then Elizabeth might have been able to forgive a small measure of flirtatiousness on his part. Instead, he acted as one who was eager to escape her company and his obligations. That certainly did not endear him to Elizabeth.

As Elizabeth studied Henry Darcy, she felt someone's gaze resting upon her and looked up to lock eyes with Mr. Darcy. For some reason, his expression seemed almost sympathetic. Perhaps he was upset about his brother's rudeness. Certainly, Elizabeth had hoped she would find a man of greater character to be engaged to Jane. Perhaps he would surprise her yet.

Somehow, however, she doubted he would prove himself to be anything other than he seemed.

CHAPTER IV

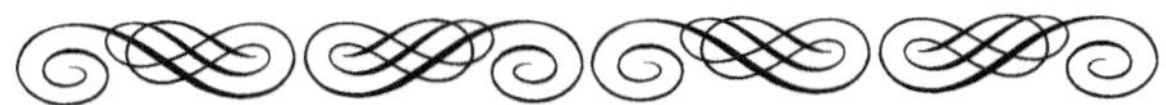

When the time arrived for Elizabeth to join the dance, she allowed Mr. Bingley to lead her to the floor. In the meantime, Mr. Darcy escorted Kitty while Henry Darcy led Jane with a wooden expression.

As they assembled on the dance floor, Elizabeth could hear people whispering nearby. Her gaze darted around to try to determine on whom their attention was focused. She could not be certain, but she thought more than one pair of eyes had rested on either Mr. Henry Darcy or Jane—or perhaps both.

Since she could not approach the strangers nearby and demand that they reveal the source of their interest, she resolved to listen carefully in hopes of gleaning even the merest scrap of information.

Mr. Bingley seemed to understand her concern, as he murmured to her: "You need not worry, for I do not believe they understand the full extent of your sister's relationship with Henry."

Elizabeth looked at the gentleman in surprise. She had not realized he was aware of the engagement. Then again, she supposed his closeness with the family could account for that. In all, she believed this to be a positive development, as she might be able to obtain some intelligence from him if she proceeded carefully.

Mr. Bingley was a pleasant dance partner, attending as he should and carrying on an easy conversation with her. She was not surprised to find him well-versed in the moves of the dance and as amiable on the dance floor as he was off it.

As a result of his amicability, Elizabeth felt comfortable enough to proceed in her quest to obtain information concerning Jane's fiancé.

"My sister has been surprisingly tight-lipped about her relationship with Mr. Henry Darcy," said Elizabeth. She spoke in a low voice but refrained from using the word "engagement" to avoid unnecessary attention.

Mr. Bingley frowned at her statement and gave a short nod. "I am not surprised to hear of her reticence."

"Do you know anything of Mr. Henry Darcy's estate?"

"Henry's estate, Haskett Hall, can be found in Leicestershire. It is small compared to Darcy's estate—that is, Pemberley, which is located in Derbyshire—and is not nearly as impressive."

Mr. Bingley must have seen the disappointed look on Elizabeth's face, as he hastened to assure her: "But though it may need some work, I believe it has potential enough. It would be unreasonable to expect the estate to be comparable to Pemberley. I rather believe very few estates in England can claim such a thing. Furthermore, Henry is not home often enough to tend to Haskett Hall as he should. That may . . . that may change in the future, of course."

Elizabeth knew he meant that the situation could change once Henry Darcy married.

She took in a deep breath, the air catching in her chest. "Mr. Bingley, forgive me for my frankness, but will his . . . his future wife be happy there?"

Mr. Bingley faltered. "She—it—that is, I do not think I can speak to that, Miss Bennet. But I hope that his wife will have only happiness in her future."

Elizabeth could have been imagining it, but she thought her question caused Mr. Bingley some distress. She wondered whether there was a reason for it, and she considered pressing the issue, but she ultimately decided not to pry. She supposed the middle of a dance floor was not the proper place for such a conversation anyway.

Moments later, however, Mr. Bingley managed one brief, albeit quiet, outburst:

"Miss Bennet, please watch over your sister."

"Could you please explain your meaning, Mr. Bingley?" asked Elizabeth quietly, feeling more than mildly alarmed.

Mr. Bingley gave only a sharp jerk of his head and averted his eyes.

Elizabeth nearly pressed him further, but she did not know whether he could not speak of what he meant or whether their current circumstances merely made further conversation inappropriate.

As the dance brought Elizabeth briefly closer to Jane and Mr. Henry Darcy, she took a moment to observe them. There still did not appear to be any spark between them. Jane wore a guarded expression, and her fiancé had the slightly petulant look of a young boy who had been forced to play with a small girl whom he had no desire to approach.

Elizabeth and Mr. Bingley engaged in little other discourse during the rest of the set. Mr. Bingley appeared to regret his words, and Elizabeth remained preoccupied with her concern for Jane. Both felt relief when the set finished, and as Mr. Bingley led Elizabeth back to Lady Catherine, Elizabeth decided she would pull Jane aside for private conversation even if it offended her ladyship. She noted with a small measure of relief that Mr. and Mrs. Gardiner were nowhere to be seen; no doubt the card tables and refreshments had proven themselves too tempting. That would simply make it easier for her to act.

Fortunately for Elizabeth's designs, Lady Catherine had become caught up in conversation with a young lady—apparently, a woman for whom Lady Catherine had served as patroness before taking Jane under her wing—and Elizabeth had only to contend with Jane's reluctance to be parted from Lady Catherine.

At last, Elizabeth succeeded in drawing Jane out of the immediate hearing of Lady Catherine, though not out of sight.

"My dear Jane," whispered Elizabeth, "is there anything with which I must be concerned? Might you wish to tell me anything in private about your fiancé or your situation in London that you would not otherwise desire to discuss?"

"You need not be concerned, Lizzy," came Jane's short reply after the barest of pauses.

"That has not been my impression of the situation," said Elizabeth. "Rather—"

She was forced to cut off due to the sudden intrusion of Mrs. Livingston, who immediately sought to compliment Jane with: "You made a fine figure on the dance floor, as always, Jane."

Jane demurred and passed on her own compliments to Mrs. Livingston.

Elizabeth, knowing her plans had been foiled for the present, gazed at the newcomer and forced herself to concentrate on making polite conversation.

"Mrs. Livingston," said she, "your brother is quite the gentleman."

"Charles is the consummate gentleman," said Mrs. Livingston with a proud smile, "but it is nearly time for him to put down roots. I keep advising him to select a bride and purchase an estate, but he has proven himself oddly reticent. Regardless, I have high hopes for his marital prospects. My husband has a particular friend whose daughter would make him an excellent match. However, my brother, to his detriment, can be stubborn when he desires, and I do not believe he fully comprehends what the best course for him would be."

Though doubtful that Caroline Livingston could ever agree with her brother on what sort of match would be ideal for him, much less what the best course for him would be, Elizabeth only smiled and replied:

"It is often easier to know what should have been done when given the gift of hindsight. Perhaps one day, some years into the future, you shall decide that your brother made the correct decisions for his own life."

From Mrs. Livingston's expression, she could never do something as scandalous as supporting her brother's every decision, but she seemed disinclined to protest the matter.

When Mr. Henry Darcy came to collect Elizabeth to lead her to the floor, she felt afire with worry and something fiercer than mere curiosity.

"Have you often been able to avail yourself of the opportunity to dance in London?" asked Mr. Henry Darcy shortly after the dance began. "You appear to be well-acquainted with the steps of the dance."

"London is not the only place with a ballroom," said Elizabeth curtly. "Even country society provides opportunities to assemble for the purpose of dancing."

"Had you a dance instructor then?"

"Mr. Darcy, is it your pride that leads you to ask such questions? If you must know, my sisters and I were given access to as many masters as were necessary, but we were commonly left to tend to ourselves and learn as much as we would. Fortunately, Jane, as the eldest, received the finest education among us, and her kind and elegant tutelage could not but serve as a boon to us all. Of course, I suspect I could extoll all of Jane's virtues to you without it causing your opinion of her to change a jot."

"I am certain your sister's character is as you say," said Mr. Henry Darcy, refusing to rise to the bait. There had been a certain flash in his eyes, however, that indicated his irritation.

Elizabeth decided to try a different tactic to induce the young man to reveal the sorts of details she wished to learn. She spoke quietly and only when the dance brought them close together, however, knowing this was not the most appropriate conversation for a ballroom.

"From what I have seen," said she, "there are some men and women in the room who appear to take an unusual interest in your relationship with my sister."

"From my experience, people are gossips and take interest in anything even mildly out of the ordinary."

"When you refer to people's perception of something as being out of the ordinary," whispered Elizabeth furiously, "do you perhaps refer to a disparity between your situation and that of my sister? I know the fact that you are related to an earl might elevate you in certain circles, and I am also aware there are some who must have noticed something unusual about your attention to my sister, as you scarcely seem to like her, much less admire her. Certainly, I know there are many who would expect you to make a different match. I do not say a *better* match, for I am convinced there is no better person in all of England than Jane."

"I am aware of the reason that I find myself in my current situation," said Mr. Henry Darcy.

The man's words struck Elizabeth as odd, but before she could request clarification, he had begun to speak again.

"You seem to know much of my family's history," said he, "especially considering you do not typically move in London society."

"My sister's happiness means the world to me," murmured Elizabeth. "It is only natural that I would want to learn more about you."

Henry Darcy laughed abruptly, causing a startled Elizabeth to look up at him.

"I like you, Miss Bennet," said he. He lowered his voice then and spoke in a teasing tone. "Perhaps it would have been better had I been engaged to *you* instead."

"You do not know what sort of angel you are receiving in Jane," said Elizabeth, favoring him with a look of disgust.

"I never asked for an angel," said the man beneath his breath. He then proceeded to drop the conversation instead of saying anything further.

Elizabeth did not resume the conversation herself, too irritated to maintain any semblance of politeness with Mr. Henry Darcy. She did not understand how this man could claim to love her sister. And if he did not love Jane, then why had he and Jane become engaged?

The mystery had been one she could not unravel despite her best attempts. Even before leaving Longbourn to stay with Lady Catherine, Jane had remained unwilling to speak about her engagement, and Elizabeth's knowledge had thus remained limited. She knew that Henry Darcy and Jane had met the previous year in London when Jane and Mr. Bennet had left to attend to some business with the Gardiners. The trip itself had seemed rather odd, for Elizabeth had expected to be invited along as well. Mr. Bennet had never made a secret of his dislike of London, and he often enjoyed having Elizabeth, his favorite daughter, nearby to make London more bearable. However, Elizabeth had not been encouraged to come—quite the opposite in fact.

Furthermore, Mr. Bennet had even turned down Mrs. Bennet's vocal pleas for her and the rest of her daughters to be allowed to accompany him. As the redcoats had not been in the area at the time, the notion of staying at home had held no appeal for Mrs. Bennet. Still, Mr. Bennet had refused to bring the rest of the family with him, and when he and Jane finally returned, it had been with the announcement of an engagement. Mrs. Bennet had been so surprised by the news that she forgot to complain about having been left behind. When she had recovered from the shock, her excitement had scarcely been containable. Upon learning the engagement was to be kept secret for undisclosed reasons, her displeasure had been just as great. If there were one thing Mrs. Bennet could not condone, it was the keeping of secrets.

For whatever reason, the engagement had been enshrouded in mystery. Still, Elizabeth would not let that discourage her when the happiness of a most beloved sister was at stake. She would do whatever she could to assist Jane, even if it meant she offended a few sensibilities along the way.

Chapter V

When Mr. Darcy arrived to collect Elizabeth as his dance partner, her mood had only worsened. The smile she proffered was weak, and the words she spoke were not much stronger.

"Do you . . . often travel to see your uncle and aunt in London?" asked Mr. Darcy. He smiled at her as one who was determined to be friendly, yet there was an awkwardness to his speech that indicated he was unaccustomed to—or uncomfortable with—making small talk.

"Not as often as I would like," said Elizabeth, attempting to calm herself and attend to her dance partner. "My father would count himself fortunate if he were never required to step foot in London again."

"Does he dislike the crowds or the atmosphere?"

"A little of both, I suppose. He prefers a more limited company. He exercises his mind by employing his powers of observation on an individual level, studying a person's foibles and teasing out the less than flattering aspects of that person's character. The more extreme a person's words and actions, the fonder he is of making his or her acquaintance—provided, of course, he is able to escape quickly if needed."

"You sound fond of your father."

"I am," said Elizabeth with a smile. "He may perhaps have been inattentive at times when it came to raising my sisters and me, but we have not felt any lack in a general sense."

The dance took them apart briefly, but when they returned together, Elizabeth looked closely at Mr. Darcy, sensing an opportunity. "Are you fond of your brother?"

"Are we not all in possession of some degree of fondness for the members of our family?"

It was not, Elizabeth realized, a direct answer to the question. She pursed her lips and then tried again to obtain more information on Mr. Henry Darcy.

"Are you aware of the particulars concerning your brother's acquaintance with . . . my family?"

"I am aware of only a few details," said Mr. Darcy in reply.

Elizabeth studied his face, but the man did not betray his inner thoughts. Perhaps she should be glad at his efforts to redirect the conversation, as it indicated a necessary circumspection. The engagement between Jane and Mr. Darcy's brother was, after all, meant to be kept private at present.

The notion that everyone but Elizabeth was privy to some secret concerning the circumstances of the engagement was beginning to gain more ground, but since a ballroom was not an appropriate place for any such secret to be unearthed, she resolved to quit her current line of questioning for the time being.

"Mr. Bingley had high praise for Pemberley," said Elizabeth, changing the subject.

A flicker of relief flashed over Mr. Darcy's face, to be replaced with something like pride. "Bingley has inquired more than once as to whether there is a figure that could convince me to part with my estate."

"Might I inquire as to what your response was?"

The pride in Mr. Darcy's face could not be mistaken now. "I told him all the money in England could not convince me to part with it."

Elizabeth laughed. "It is a marvel, then, that he continues to pester you."

"I think Bingley's persistence is more of a testament to the greatness of the estate than any tenacity on Bingley's part."

"You must truly love your home."

"I do."

Elizabeth tilted her head as she regarded him. Both the warmth in his voice as he spoke of Pemberley and the slight smile that touched his lips transformed him, wiping away any traces of awkwardness. She suspected he could wax eloquent on his estate with little prodding. She was much the same with regard to her beloved walking paths at Longbourn; in that, she and Mr. Darcy seemed to be kindred spirits.

"Your brother must benefit greatly from your estate knowledge," said Elizabeth.

"I suppose," said Mr. Darcy in return.

Elizabeth could feel him withdrawing from her due to the reference to his brother, so she cast about for a different subject. "When you spoke of your sister earlier, there was a certain softness to your features that seemed to indicate a particular fondness for her."

"I am indeed fond of Georgiana," said the gentleman warmly. "In many ways, she is much like me, for she possesses a natural reticence that makes her uncomfortable in strange company. She is not yet out, and while Henry believes she should be, the decision does not rest on him. Rather, my cousin, Colonel Fitzwilliam, shares the guardianship of Georgiana with me. As my father passed away six years ago, following the death of my mother, I was scarcely of age myself to take over Georgiana's guardianship; Henry certainly was not."

"I suppose your sister must have been quite young at the time," said Elizabeth tentatively.

"There is a difference of twelve years between us," said Mr. Darcy, "so she was but ten at the time."

"It must have been difficult for her to lose her parents at so young an age," said Elizabeth. As she spoke, however, she looked on Mr. Darcy with sympathy, knowing it must have been difficult for him as well.

"Their deaths were a great blow to us all," said he, confirming her thoughts. "When my father was alive, Henry would have found a way to turn dust to gold had my father only requested it of him, and I scarcely felt ready for the guardianship of my siblings, much less the other responsibilities that had been thrust upon me. I fear Georgiana had the worst of it, though, for what could I, a young man, have known about raising a girl to adulthood?"

Mr. Darcy glanced at Elizabeth suddenly, as if he realized he had spoken his innermost thoughts aloud. He turned his head away, and then, in a tone meant to lighten the emotion of the conversation, he said: "I understand your parents are no strangers to the trials and tribulations of raising a young woman."

Willing to allow the conversation to touch on less sensitive matters, Elizabeth said: "As there are five Bennet daughters, my parents can claim intimate knowledge of the hardships involved in raising girls. Jane provided them no difficulties, of course, but I must have been quite a bit more work for them. Mary is the third-born, and she is more interested in creating moral extracts and practicing the pianoforte than in pursuing lace or dance partners. Kitty and Lydia, however, have proven themselves to be much more challenging. Though Lydia is the youngest, Kitty tends to follow Lydia in whatever she does. I believe their current separation will serve to benefit both of them."

Though she had spoken more than she had intended, Elizabeth supposed it only proper that Mr. Darcy become better acquainted with the personalities of her sisters.

"I suppose not every family has the benefit of two male heirs," said she with a smile.

"Indeed," said Mr. Darcy, giving her a serious look. "I understand there is an entail on your family's estate."

"Your understanding is correct," replied Elizabeth. "It was my mother's favorite topic to bemoan until Jane's engagement came about, and for that very reason, I am not surprised to find you aware of it. Fortunately, my mother is much quieter about it now."

An odd expression came over Mr. Darcy's face. "Yes, I suppose the engagement did much to relieve your family's burden."

After witnessing the man's reaction to her words, Elizabeth chastised herself for the intimacy of their conversation. Even though the man was to be her brother, he was still a new acquaintance, and she should have been heeding her words around him. Someone who did not know Jane well could find it easy to believe her to be the calculating and greedy sort of woman who chased men of great fortune in hopes of ensnaring one of them, but such an opinion could not be further from the truth. While Elizabeth did not know Jane's reasons for marrying Mr. Henry Darcy, Elizabeth *did* know that it would not have been due to entrapment of any sort on Jane's part.

She wished to trumpet Jane's character—to proclaim that Jane had never been the sort to pursue a man solely for his fortune—but she pushed aside the impulse with some effort and turned the conversation to a less sensitive topic.

The rest of the evening passed in a relatively agreeable fashion. Henry Darcy did eventually deign to ask Kitty to dance with him, though Elizabeth, who had seen a somber Mr. Darcy in a quiet but firm conversation with his brother, suspected it had only been due to well-meaning interference. Still, regardless of the reason, Kitty had been pleased to accept the request, and while Mr. Henry Darcy's expression had been distant and reminiscent of distaste, the circumstances did not dampen Kitty's mood.

In fact, though Mr. Henry Darcy must have served as only the most rudimentary of dance partners, Kitty appeared almost ecstatic when she returned from the dance to join Elizabeth, Jane, and Mrs. Livingston.

Mr. Henry Darcy smiled archly at Elizabeth before he took his leave of the four young women.

"La!" said Kitty. "What a fine dance partner he made! He is a very handsome man in a roguish sort of way, and he lacks the stodginess I so dislike. Jane, you are fortunate that such a man is in love with you! If you were not my sister, I would be determined to steal him away from you!"

Jane mumbled something unintelligible in response. However, before either Kitty or Elizabeth could ask what she had said, Caroline Livingston spoke.

"Jane shall be the perfect mistress for Haskett Hall. I will own that the estate may need a little work, but I do not doubt that she is up to the task. I believe a slightly younger mistress would not do nearly so well; rather, having someone who bears Jane's maturity is paramount."

Though Mrs. Livingston's words appeared to be in part a veiled insult toward Kitty, they did elevate Jane. They also revealed knowledge that Elizabeth had not known Mrs. Livingston possessed.

Elizabeth tilted her head in surprise. Of course, she supposed that Mrs. Livingston's knowledge of the engagement could be attributed to either Mrs. Livingston's closeness with Jane or Mr. Bingley's closeness with Mr. Darcy. The woman's words about the estate, however, gave her pause. Based on what she had heard thus far, she would not be surprised to find Haskett Hall in utter shambles. What sort of work needed to be done to restore it? Would the work even be worth undertaking? Would Jane be able to institute whatever changes were necessary, or would any actions be hopeless?

The rest of the night did little to elucidate Elizabeth as to what sort of future awaited her beloved sister.

CHAPTER VI

A few days after the ball, Lady Catherine announced her decision to extend a limited part of her patronage to Elizabeth and Kitty. Elizabeth suspected Lady Catherine merely wished to ensure that the behavior of the Bennet daughters would reflect favorably on Lady Catherine's own family once Jane married Henry Darcy, but whatever the cause, Lady Catherine seemed to expect the gift of her patronage to be met with effusive gratitude.

Neither Elizabeth nor Kitty particularly desired to be in company with Lady Catherine more often than necessary, but as the unexpected development meant Elizabeth would be allowed to see Jane more often, she expressed the appropriate amount of gratitude to satisfy her ladyship's desire for praise.

Elizabeth's attempt to placate Lady Catherine met with results almost immediately, for the woman invited Elizabeth and Kitty to join her, Jane, and the two male Darcys in their private box at the opera. Her ladyship noted with an uncharacteristically apologetic air that she would have invited the Gardiners as well, but the opera box only seated six. The Gardiners had discussed the invitation briefly and agreed that Elizabeth and Kitty could be entrusted to Lady Catherine for the performance; after all, they could scarcely deny Lady

Catherine's ability to watch over the two young women when her ladyship had already been given leave to guide Jane in London.

Much to Elizabeth's exasperation (and Mr. Henry Darcy's, if his snort were anything to go by), Lady Catherine insisted that Jane sit between her and Henry Darcy. She then arranged the seating of the rest of the box's inhabitants, thus leading Elizabeth to her current placement beside Mr. Darcy.

"You must forgive my aunt, Miss Elizabeth," said Mr. Darcy, speaking in a soft voice as he leaned toward Elizabeth. "My cousin Anne was sick for a long time before she finally passed away. My aunt's desire for control has only grown stronger since. My aunt was also close to my mother, after whom Anne was named, so my mother's death had a great impact as well."

Glancing at Lady Catherine, Elizabeth felt her opinions of the woman soften. Lady Catherine had already lost a husband, a daughter, and a sister. Perhaps she was due some sympathy. Surely Elizabeth could overlook *some* of her officiousness.

Elizabeth met Mr. Darcy's eyes and gave a slight nod of acknowledgment. He must have seen her sincerity, as he offered a tight smile before straightening and settling back in his seat.

While many of those present at the opera frequently moved about and conversed during the performance, Elizabeth had always preferred to concentrate on what was before her. She would watch the performers with rapt attention, attempting to capture every nuance of sound despite the general inattentiveness of some of the men and women near her.

At least, Elizabeth typically behaved in such a fashion when attending an opera. This time, however, she found herself distracted several times. One of the two main distractions was Lady Catherine's voice. Her ladyship appeared to be determined to maintain a critical or expositive commentary, whether she was talking about the costumes of the players or the identity of patrons in nearby boxes. These remarks were focused at times on Jane and at times on Kitty. As Kitty occupied a seat on the row behind her ladyship, this required a lot of twisting and craning of the neck on Lady Catherine's part, not to mention a certain level of loudness.

The other distraction Elizabeth faced was the relationship between Henry Darcy and Jane—or rather, the lack thereof.

A relationship between two people in love, as she had supposed Jane and Mr. Henry Darcy to have been, should have manifested itself in some way—perhaps through a few furtive glances, a shy smile, or even just an inclination to remain in company together. However, Henry Darcy had the reluctant appearance of a man who wished to escape his present company entirely, and Jane herself remained quiet and withdrawn. Even Kitty, whom Elizabeth would never have identified as being someone with powers of discernment, kept glancing at the two in obvious puzzlement.

Elizabeth wished to ply Mr. Darcy with questions—*Could Henry Darcy ever grow to love Jane? Was he in love with another woman? How had two such dissimilar people come to be engaged with one another?*—but knowing she and Mr. Darcy had not reached the appropriate level of intimacy to enable her to ask such questions, Elizabeth refrained from speaking.

By the time intermission came, Elizabeth felt stifled by the air in the private box, and she gladly allowed Lady Catherine to sweep her and the box's other occupants down to the lobby.

If Elizabeth had hoped to speak to Jane, she was to be sorely disappointed, as Lady Catherine dominated Jane's company from the moment they stepped into the lobby, facilitating various introductions with those she deemed worthy of notice. Elizabeth and Kitty were included in these introductions, but the majority of Lady Catherine's praise fell on Jane. Elizabeth supposed some part of her should be proud that Jane had gained even Lady Catherine's approbation, but she merely felt agitated.

"If you will please pardon me," said Henry Darcy with an exaggerated bow to his aunt, "I see some people with whom I must speak."

"Nonsense, Henry," said Lady Catherine. "You must stay, for there are those here who would wish to speak with you, and I count myself as being among their number."

The man's lip twitched, and Elizabeth could only imagine the remarks he had to bite back. He remained in place, however, though it seemed likely he would not do so for long.

Elizabeth, who stood at the edge of their group (and beside the impeccably dressed couple whose attention Lady Catherine currently commanded), glanced around to observe the crowd. She noticed several sets of eyes on her party, though she could not blame them for their curiosity. Lady Catherine made quite the sight with her elaborate feather headdress and her towering height.

As Elizabeth continued to gaze at the people nearby, however, she noticed a few men and women whispering and staring at Henry Darcy and Jane. The faces of these strangers were difficult to read due to the mixed emotions upon them, and Elizabeth wished she knew what was being said.

One woman nearby spoke behind a hand to another woman, her narrowed eyes alternating between Mr. Henry Darcy and Jane. The second woman gave a curt shake of her head and murmured something in response.

"Do you enjoy opera, Miss Elizabeth?" asked Mr. Darcy suddenly.

Elizabeth felt a flash of irritation at the interruption, but the feeling passed quickly. As the gentleman had good intentions, she should offer him a pleasant response.

"I do," said she. "While I am not so fluent in Italian that I understand every word sung, I allow the emotions of those on stage and the feelings engendered by the music to fill in any gaps in my knowledge."

Mr. Darcy gave her a slight smile. "I have long been of the impression that music transcends language."

"My thoughts are in accord with yours on the subject, then," said Elizabeth. "Music is a language of its own. You can learn much about people by observing how they approach different pieces of music. A diligent and serious sort might play with technical proficiency but no real emotion, whereas a more playful type might spend less time practicing but expend more effort into bringing out the intended mood of the music."

"I suppose I could venture a guess as to which sort of musician you view yourself as."

"Were you to guess that I am the playful sort, then you would be correct. To my detriment, I have never ventured to practice as often as I ought. Of course, whether anyone receives pleasure from my playing is something I cannot say."

"I am certain there are none who would say otherwise."

Elizabeth only gave a demure smile in response.

Kitty, who stood near Elizabeth, appeared to have forgotten that they were among acquaintances, as she interrupted the conversation between her sister and Mr. Darcy to say none too quietly: "Lizzy, I cannot understand this at all. From the way they behave, you would not think that Jane and Mr. Henry Darcy even *like* each other, much less *love* each other."

Elizabeth flushed in embarrassment and admonished her sister quietly with: "Kitty! Please mind your tongue."

She gave Mr. Darcy an apologetic look, unable to conjure up the appropriate words to smooth over her younger sister's blunder. The gentleman's countenance could not be read easily as he gazed back at her, but he seemed almost troubled.

Gathering her thoughts together and knowing she must speak at least a few words, Elizabeth said, ostensibly to Kitty, "Affection may be expressed in a multitude of ways that are not always easily discernible."

Kitty murmured something in response, and rather than ask her to repeat herself, Elizabeth endeavored to turn the conversation to a new subject.

"Mr. Darcy, have you and Mr. Bingley known each other for a long time?" asked Elizabeth. Though Mr. Bingley had not accompanied them to the opera, Elizabeth had become accustomed to seeing him, and she thought their group felt the loss of his ebullience.

"We have been friends since school," said Mr. Darcy. "He has never been fond of opera, and I suppose our opinions on many subjects are not in alignment, yet his joviality makes recompense for my unfortunate taciturnity."

"I have not witnessed any such failure on your part, for you have been quite willing to engage in discourse with me."

The man inclined his head. "Certainly, I feel more comfortable when surrounded by people whom I know or circumstances with which I am familiar. However, I suspect you might find me frightful in Hertfordshire society."

"That is not a problem at all," said Kitty to Mr. Darcy. "Much like my father, Lizzy enjoys character studies, so she might find you even more interesting if you were less pleasant."

Elizabeth gave a broad smile. "I fear my sister has the right of it, Mr. Darcy. However, based on even the little that I know of you, I fear you are not the sort to be teased with impunity."

"I suspect that few people enjoy being teased," said Mr. Darcy.

"I am afraid I must disagree with you," said Elizabeth, "for if we cannot make light of ourselves, then the world around us becomes heavy indeed."

She found herself distracted by the sudden sight of Henry Darcy extricating himself from Lady Catherine's hold and beginning to push his way through the crowd. Though he could have been eager to converse with some school fellows or a casual acquaintance, Elizabeth suspected he instead meant to find some willing young woman with whom to speak.

Fortunately, she was not so caught up in watching him that she missed Mr. Darcy's words.

"I suppose that if you are so willing to tease others," said he, "then you must take a great deal of pleasure in being teased yourself."

By this point, Elizabeth could no longer see Mr. Henry Darcy, so she reluctantly turned her full attention to Mr. Darcy. "I suppose, as a rule, much of the pleasure to be found in teasing is dependent upon the recipient's relationship with the one doing the teasing. I know I should much prefer to be laughed at by a close friend or valued acquaintance than a mere stranger."

"I suppose my own pride precludes any enjoyment from being teased by anyone."

Elizabeth tilted her head. "You might be an exception to the general rule, Mr. Darcy. I suspect that if you are in the company of a person whom you highly value, you would rather be teased by that person than praised by another."

"I suppose I should not venture to contradict an intelligent young woman such as yourself," said the man with a smile.

"You would do well to refrain from such an attitude, Mr. Darcy," said Kitty, "for Elizabeth is known to occasionally spout opinions that are not her own."

"You need not provide Mr. Darcy with such insights so early in our acquaintance, Kitty," said Elizabeth teasingly.

"Henry?" came Lady Catherine's voice, causing Elizabeth to turn and look at her. "Wherever did that young man disappear to?"

After her ladyship had searched their immediate vicinity, she moved toward Elizabeth, Kitty, and Mr. Darcy, demanding to know whether they were in possession of knowledge concerning Henry Darcy's location. Though Elizabeth had seen him leave their group, she had no idea of his current whereabouts, and she joined the others in indicating such.

Lady Catherine huffed in vexation. "That young man tries my patience, but I suppose there is nothing to be done about it. Let us return to the box. Perhaps he shall deign to join us there."

Elizabeth, who wished to take a few minutes in the retiring room, indicated she would return to the box shortly. She then parted with her company and made her way through the crowd to reach her destination.

After exiting the retiring room a few minutes later, she paused when she noticed Henry Darcy speaking with a young woman nearby. Their flirtation could not have been mistaken as anything else due to their laughter and smiles, and Henry Darcy soon began to lean much too close to the woman, his expression almost leering.

A woman of a weaker disposition or a less-developed sense of morality might have merely passed by the pair and allowed their flirtation to continue, but Elizabeth was no such woman, and the fires of her righteous anger roared to life at the sight. She would not allow Henry Darcy to further trample all over his relationship with Jane if she could prevent it.

Elizabeth approached the chuckling pair with a martial stiffness and grated out: "Mr. Darcy." She resisted giving the woman a frosty look, for the woman likely did not know that Henry Darcy was engaged, but she had no such compunction with treating the man himself coldly.

The lady giggled, presumably missing the irritated aura emanating from Elizabeth. Unsurprisingly, the woman seemed as if she had more beauty than sense.

Henry Darcy let loose a sigh and turned a suffering look on Elizabeth as he prepared to make the introductions. "Miss Bennet, this is the lovely, ah . . . Dorothea Carter." His pause indicated he had briefly forgotten the young woman's name. "Miss Carter, this is Miss Elizabeth Bennet."

Elizabeth pursed her lips, none too impressed by his introductions but also not desiring to extend them, and then she said: "Mr. Darcy, the rest of our party awaits your presence. I fear you will have to make your apologies to Miss Carter."

Henry Darcy took a moment to observe the look of determination upon Elizabeth's face as she stared him down. He then presumably realized that she would not be gainsaid, as he said: "Miss Carter, I fear it is as Miss Bennet says, and I may not tarry. Still, you need not fear the sorrow of our parting, for I am certain we shall meet again."

Miss Carter tittered. "I do hope so."

The gentleman favored her with a warm smile before offering his arm to Elizabeth. "Shall we, Miss Bennet?"

Though fuming, Elizabeth took the proffered arm. She would not meet civility with incivility.

Moments after they had begun to walk away, Henry Darcy murmured: "I am beginning to suspect that you dislike me, Miss Bennet."

Not wanting to destroy relations with her future brother-in-law, Elizabeth swallowed the scathing reply that rose to her throat and said instead: "I merely think that you need to learn your place."

The man gave a mirthless laugh. "That is interesting to hear coming from someone such as you."

His words raised Elizabeth's ire, and her tentative control of her temper threatened to dissolve. "I suppose you are referring to the states of our families. Well, Jane and I are both daughters of a gentleman, just as you are the son of a gentleman. In that sense, there is no inequality to be found.

"The difference between us, however, is that my sister and I are fully aware of the strictures of propriety and know that proper behavior does not consist of pursuing a myriad of dalliances for the mere purpose of collecting them as some women collect brooches and bracelets. I might suggest that you pay more heed to *Jane* and less attention to the empty-headed *flirts* whose siren calls shall bring you naught but trouble."

Henry Darcy smirked but said nothing in response, as they had nearly reached their company in the box.

When the moment arrived for Elizabeth to relinquish her grip on the man's arm, she did so with the celerity of a person releasing an unexpectedly slimy object.

"Henry, I am not certain we would have seen you again if not for Miss Elizabeth," said Lady Catherine. "I shall never understand why you are so fond of disappearing at events such as this."

After Henry Darcy made some sort of muttered reply, his brother looked at Elizabeth. "Miss Elizabeth, are you well?"

She glanced at him as she moved toward her seat, only to find her steps arrested at the expression of mild alarm on his face. Were her emotions so obvious?

"I am as well as I can be under the circumstances," murmured she before proceeding to seat herself. She could sense his eyes on her, but she could not trust herself to say anything further, and he did not press the issue.

CHAPTER VII

For Elizabeth, the London social scene remained busy, mystifying, and vexing. Caroline Livingston and Lady Catherine both continued to dominate much of Jane's time, with the former whispering as if she and Jane shared secrets of the utmost significance and the latter pontificating as if all the world could benefit from the continual receipt of her wisdom. In contrast to Lady Catherine's attitude, Mr. Bingley continued to display a level of hesitance that indicated he wished to tell Elizabeth something he could not manage to put to words. As if those attitudes would not have been frustrating enough by themselves, the whispers of the crowds persevered. Though Elizabeth had determined that the whispers did not seem to be directly focused on Jane, their very existence agitated Elizabeth.

A person of lesser determination might have given up and returned home, but Elizabeth insisted to Mrs. Gardiner that she intended to persist in investigating the circumstances surrounding Jane's engagement. Fortunately, the answer to most of her questions soon came from an unexpected source.

Elizabeth was seated in the drawing-room at Lady Catherine's townhouse with her ladyship and Jane when the former made an abrupt proclamation.

"Miss Bennet," said Lady Catherine, "your current hairstyle is not very becoming. You do not possess ringlets so much as a myriad of flat strands utterly devoid of life. You cannot merely trust yourself to the hands of a servant, you know. You must be certain to check each servant's work to ensure any assigned tasks have been performed to your satisfaction. This shall, of course, become even more important once you become the mistress of an estate, but you must form the habit now, or the servants shall trample all over you as a horse tramples over the grass beneath its feet."

Jane opened her mouth as if she were about to apologize, but Lady Catherine commanded, "Come, Miss Bennet," and then she all but dragged Jane from the room, no doubt intending to personally oversee the correction of the young woman's hairstyle.

Elizabeth returned her attention to the embroidery she had in hand, but not too long afterward, she found herself with an unexpected guest.

"Mr. Darcy," said she in surprise.

"Miss Bennet," returned he, his gaze traveling around the room. He seemed surprised to find her alone, as he merely stood in place awkwardly, his eyes meeting Elizabeth's briefly before darting away. He then took a deep breath and appeared to be about to take his leave, but Elizabeth stopped him.

"Mr. Darcy," said she almost plaintively.

"Yes, Miss Bennet?"

"As someone who is slated to be my brother-in-law, you should understand that I expect truthfulness from you," began she.

His face darkened. "Disguise of any kind is my abhorrence, Miss Bennet."

"Then you will have no scruples in taking a moment to answer my questions honestly," said she, her eyes resting pointedly on a nearby sofa.

He hesitated and then followed her cue, walking over and seating himself nearby.

"Mr. Darcy," said she quietly, "I have seen how strangely people act around your brother. While their attention is not confined to his relationship with Jane, she has earned her share of staring through her obvious association with him. Please tell me, Mr. Darcy, why people seem so concerned about your brother."

The gentleman remained silent for several heartbeats, and Elizabeth began to wonder whether he intended to answer at all. Finally, however, he found the words he desired.

"Miss Bennet," said he, "I would normally never consider broaching such a topic with a young woman, but I believe it is better that you know the full truth now rather than later. My brother—"

He ceased speaking abruptly, his brow furrowing as he attempted to gather his thoughts once more.

"Mr. Darcy," said Elizabeth, "you may speak frankly with me without fear that I shall be offended. My sensibilities are not so strong that I shall faint at something you might have to say, even if it is not meant for polite company."

The corner of Mr. Darcy's lip lifted briefly, but his countenance was so grave that it seemed more of a grimace than a smile. "My younger brother . . . That is . . ."

Elizabeth watched as Mr. Darcy struggled to find words. Despite her impatience, she did not pressure him but instead allowed him to proceed haltingly.

"My brother is a rake of . . . questionable morality. I fear his behavior with women and his gambling have led to the necessity for some people to be . . . encouraged to remain circumspect."

Mr. Darcy must have seen the glint in Elizabeth's eyes that indicated her intent to reply, as he hurried to say more. "I have tried to talk to him, Miss Bennet. Numerous times have I tried lecturing, cajoling, and even begging him to mend his ways. I have told him that your sister deserves better and that he ought to strive to be a better man for *her sake*, if no one else's, but my words have had no effect. He is not to be swayed. He considers his marriage to your eldest sister to be unwanted and unavoidable, yet he still will not effect any changes in himself.

"I have attempted to do all that I can, but to no avail. Miss Bennet, I think perhaps—that is, I would strongly encourage you to ask your sister to break off the engagement."

For Mr. Darcy to speak of the faults of his brother so openly indicated the serious nature of the present situation. Elizabeth believed him when he claimed he had attempted to change his brother's ways, and she also believed that Mr. Henry Darcy was the sort who would answer to no person except himself.

Unfortunately, Henry Darcy was not the only one in possession of a stubborn streak. Jane had such a streak of her own, though hers was as unselfish as his was selfish.

"I would like nothing more than to do what you say," said Elizabeth. "However, even if I should manage to spend a month alone with my sister, I would never be able to convince her to dissolve the engagement. Jane takes self-sacrifice to greater heights than you might imagine. Even though her engagement to your brother remains a secret from the public, she would never break an engagement for fear of damaging her family's reputation. Furthermore, she is the sort to attribute all manner of goodness to people who have none, so even if she might face a miserable future with your brother, she would never say anything ill of him.

"To be frank, Mr. Darcy, I believe your time would be better spent entreating your brother to break the engagement himself. He obviously fails to see Jane's worth, and even if some of those who have seen him in London might think he has been specifically courting Jane, his cessation of such should not have any lasting effect due to your family's reputation."

Mr. Darcy did not respond, and Elizabeth shook her head in mystification as she considered the present circumstances. "In fact, I do not know how they came to be engaged in the first place. Are you aware of some sort of scandal, Mr. Darcy, or something that happened with the potential for scandal? That is the only explanation of which I have been able to conceive as being within the realm of possibility. My sister has refused to give me any details."

Still, Mr. Darcy remained quiet, his expression as inscrutable as stone.

At his silence, Elizabeth felt her irritation grow. "Even if you will not enlighten me as to any particulars, can you deny that it would be best for your brother to be the one to bring an end to this? Surely you do not fear that the vaunted Darcy reputation might somehow suffer if you entreat your brother to end the engagement."

Mr. Darcy studied her face for a few moments before he spoke. "Do you truly wish for the engagement between Miss Bennet and my brother to be dissolved? You must be aware of the advantage that their marriage would bring to you and your sisters, not to mention the security that a Bennet daughter's marriage to a Darcy would bring in light of the entail on your father's estate."

Elizabeth scoffed. "Though my mother may complain about the entail's existence, I rarely spare it a thought. I believe Jane is so handsome and good that she is more than capable of one day attracting the notice of a worthy young gentleman. At least, such would be the case were she not already attached to your brother.

"Furthermore, Jane and I are both more than capable of becoming governesses should the need arise. I can think of worse fates than that."

"And what of your other sisters?"

Elizabeth colored. "Jane and I would find some way to aid them should the need arise. Our family has no need of Darcy charity."

"My brother would never marry someone purely for charitable reasons, if that is what you are thinking, Miss Bennet."

"If that is so, then why *are* they marrying?"

Mr. Darcy looked away. "If you, who are close to your sister, do not know, then why should I, who am decidedly not close to my brother, know much more than you do?"

"That was an evasion if I ever heard one."

The gentleman tipped his head. "I suppose I cannot deny it. Though I do abhor disguise of every sort, it is not my story to tell. I can, however, tell you this: the engagement is of long standing."

"Might you tell me why there is such an insistence on secrecy?"

"Mr. Bennet wished the engagement not to be widely known to give time for your sister and my brother to learn more about one another."

"Did he indeed? Could it have been that he wanted to give the two young people a chance to dissolve the engagement if desired?"

Mr. Darcy averted his eyes, leading Elizabeth to believe she had hit the mark. "I have said more than I should already, Miss Bennet."

Then, before she could attempt to extract more information from him, he took his leave.

Elizabeth turned her eyes to her needlework, but her mind rested on Jane. She was surprised to hear the engagement had been in place for some time, as Elizabeth had heard of it only recently. Of course, now that she truly considered the issue, she had to own that Jane had long avoided discussing the notion of falling in love with a suitable gentleman. Elizabeth had never known the reason for Jane's discomfort, but now she suddenly understood.

Mr. Bennet could likely name the exact date the engagement had come into place, but if he had not imparted the information to Elizabeth yet, then he likely had no intention of doing so at all.

Her thoughts returned to Mr. Darcy. She wished to be cross with him—and felt she would be justified if she were—but she supposed that he was merely attempting to refrain from revealing much of what he knew. As the elder Darcy, he likely had knowledge of most of the details concerning the engagement, if not all of them, but if Mr. Bennet had asked him to keep quiet, then he would want to honor the request.

Furthermore, he could have possessed his own reasons for remaining reserved in discussing the issue.

Upon the return of Jane and Lady Catherine, Elizabeth attempted to find a way to speak to Jane alone. An opening finally came when Lady Catherine left to deal with some matter of the servants.

"I am glad to have a moment to speak alone with you," said Elizabeth, smiling at her sister, who turned toward her. "I had something to ask you. How long have you been engaged to Mr. Henry Darcy?"

Jane turned pale, but rather than answer, she merely looked at her sister and held her silence.

"I have attempted to retain a tenuous grasp on my patience, but I simply must have answers to my questions, Jane. Why are you engaged to that man? When did your engagement begin?"

Jane gave a sad smile that tore at Elizabeth's heart. "Lizzy, those are not questions for me."

"If not for you, then who?" cried Elizabeth, throwing her hands in the air. "They are certainly not questions for Henry Darcy. I doubt *that* man would answer any of my questions out of sheer contrariness."

But Jane, dear self-sacrificing Jane, merely embraced her, whispered her love, and left the drawing-room.

Elizabeth stared after her until Lady Catherine's return, longing for a return of the feeling of closeness that had once been shared with her dearest sister.

CHAPTER VIII

Even before Elizabeth and Kitty stepped through the drawing-room doors at Lady Catherine's townhouse, Elizabeth could hear Lady Catherine lecturing Jane concerning the evening's dinner party.

"It will be a rather large party for your first venture into serving as hostess," said Lady Catherine as the two young women entered, "but the closeness of the company renders it acceptable in this instance. However, as my brother shall be present, you must comport yourself perfectly and make no mistakes."

While the presence of an earl would put pressure on Jane in spite of Lady Catherine's assistance, Elizabeth considered her ladyship's exaggerated way of speaking about the party to be quite ridiculous. The elements of hosting that would fall upon Jane were not difficult to handle or comprehend, and Jane had assisted at Longbourn with most, if not all, of the tasks on which Lady Catherine continued to lecture. Still, Elizabeth knew that her ladyship, in her own misguided way, meant well, so she did not attempt to intervene.

Jane murmured a response to her patroness, no doubt a reassurance or acknowledgment of some kind, though it was too quiet for Elizabeth to make out.

Lady Catherine, seeming satisfied, looked to Elizabeth and Kitty. Given a choice, Elizabeth might have stayed away to allow Jane to concentrate on her hosting duties, but Lady Catherine had insisted both Elizabeth and Kitty arrive early to reap the benefits of her well-meaning condescension.

"You must sit nearby, Miss Elizabeth and Miss Catherine," said Lady Catherine with an air of magnanimity, "for there is much that you might learn as well. One day, you may be mistresses of your own home, so you would do well to learn about the trials of hosting as well."

"We would be grateful to hear whatever you have to teach us," said Kitty politely, causing Elizabeth to look at her in surprise. The slight tug of a smile at Kitty's mouth, however, indicated that she had not been entirely sincere in her response.

"Certainly, you will," said Lady Catherine, gesturing for them to come closer. After Elizabeth and Kitty had seated themselves, she began to lecture once more.

A short while later, Mr. Darcy and Mr. Bingley appeared. The former needed to discuss some business with Lady Catherine that was quickly resolved, and the latter seemed content to sit in the drawing-room in relative silence, sneaking occasional looks at Jane that Elizabeth did not miss.

Once the business had been concluded, however, the gentlemen did not return to Mr. Darcy's townhouse; rather, they remained with the ladies and made polite conversation in the midst of Lady Catherine's proffering of advice to Jane.

Lady Catherine seemed determined to impart her wisdom despite her nephew's appearance, but finally, her attention was successfully diverted from her lessons by the arrival of a pair of morning callers: Mr. William Collins and his wife.

Though Mr. Collins was Elizabeth's cousin, she had no pleasant feelings toward him. Two years before, he had come to Longbourn to heal the rift that had existed between his father and Mr. Bennet, and while Mr. Bennet had held no qualms in welcoming him and all his pompous ludicrousness to Longbourn, Elizabeth had felt much less inclined to laugh over the evidence of such numerous character flaws when she found the man focused upon her with the intent to make her his wife.

Mr. Collins had ultimately left Longbourn empty-handed, but he had sent a crowing letter to Mr. Bennet once he finally found a woman willing to marry him. Mr. Bennet had read the letter to the rest of his family with obvious delight, proclaiming he wished he could meet the woman silly enough to marry Mr. Collins. Now that Elizabeth found herself in the same room as Mrs. Collins, she could only gape at how the woman's demeanor bore a startling resemblance to Lady Catherine.

"We have come to London to see my family for a short time," said Mrs. Collins to Elizabeth after introductions had been made. "I have always said that one should travel to London at least once a year, though I should never recommend doing so during the summer months. Travel during the summer, in general, should be avoided, you know; I rather think it unnecessary to expose oneself to the heat and misery of such a time. Furthermore, London is so malodorous once the summer heat begins to saturate the streets that it is nearly enough to make a well-bred lady faint."

Elizabeth glanced at Lady Catherine, whose expression seemed quite foul, and she had the distinct impression that Lady Catherine felt less than fond of Mr. Collins's bride.

Wishing to smooth over the situation, Elizabeth ventured: "I suppose I have not been to London frequently enough to be able to render such an opinion myself."

"Indeed," said Mrs. Collins. "I should not have expected that from you."

Elizabeth glanced at Jane, who remained quiet. While Jane might ordinarily have ventured to act as a mediator for the conversation between Mrs. Collins and Lady Catherine, she appeared to have no inclination to do so. It was an office Elizabeth felt ill-qualified to take on, yet she worried something catastrophic might happen if she did not. The gentlemen present were certainly of no assistance; Mr. Collins seemed content to let his wife speak for him, Mr. Darcy remained taciturn, and Mr. Bingley occupied himself in staring at Jane and worrying his lip. Unfortunately, the situation was only to worsen.

"I dare say that the sofa upon which her ladyship sits does not quite match the décor of this drawing-room," said Mrs. Collins with a pensive look. "I do recall that Mrs. Wilkins had a very airy sort of sofa that would do much better."

Lady Catherine's expression only grew darker, such that it seemed as if a thundercloud had taken up residence in her face.

"I must disagree, Mrs. Collins," said Lady Catherine. "The piece in question was chosen specifically for this room, and I believe it makes for a fine union of beauty and comfort."

"Well," said Mrs. Collins, her tone of voice just short of a huff, "perhaps if the sofa were repositioned, it would feel more suitable for the space."

"Your ladyship," interjected Mr. Collins suddenly, bowing toward Lady Catherine, "I must say that I am well-pleased to find myself in company with you once more. It has been far too long since I have had the opportunity to enjoy your noble condescension. Furthermore, I am much heartened by the fact that you are so closely involved in improving the comportment of my dear cousins as well as increasing their understanding of the world in which we live."

"Indeed," said Lady Catherine, softening.

"Certainly, it is always a pleasure to see people with whom we have been parted for some time," said Mrs. Collins, latching on to part of what her husband had said. "I know I greatly enjoy the opportunity to converse with my parents and my siblings in London. I am certain, your ladyship, that you could do nothing other than approve of my family, for there are none more admirable in all of England. You are welcome to stop by at your convenience."

"Ah, I believe her ladyship to be much too busy for making calls," said Mr. Collins hastily, his eyes darting back and forth between Lady Catherine and Mrs. Collins as he heaved a few anxious breaths.

Mrs. Collins scoffed: "Too busy to see the connections of her parson's wife? Surely not."

Elizabeth felt thoroughly embarrassed by her relations. While Lady Catherine had selected Mr. Collins to be the parson for Hunsford and could thus not speak strongly against him without causing damage to herself, Mr. Darcy and Mr. Bingley could claim no such attachment to the man. Furthermore, there could be no excuse for Mrs. Collins's rudeness.

"I understand there are certain duties inherent in Lady Catherine's position from which it is difficult to escape," said Elizabeth hastily. She glanced at Mr. Darcy and Mr. Bingley and could have sworn she saw the former fighting to hide a smile.

"Are there not duties that a clergyman must uphold?" countered Mrs. Collins. "My husband tends to his parishioners' needs in such a way that there are none who might find cause to malign him. He is as pious and intelligent and dedicated as ever a man who took up the position of parson. Such an upstanding young man and those with whom he is connected can only attract visitors as a droplet of honey attracts flies. I dare say I was wise indeed when I chose to marry such a man. My foresight for having made such a choice can only be praised."

Lady Catherine narrowed her eyes and studied the woman for a moment. "Certainly, your choice of a husband may only be commended. However, I find it incumbent upon me to remind you that I was the one who first undertook the pleasure of your husband's company. Furthermore, I made the perspicacious decision to appoint him as the master of Hunsford parsonage, the overseer of parishioners who were in need of spiritual guidance."

"I dare say that the circumstance of meeting one person before another has had the opportunity is not one that should in itself be cause for praise," said Mrs. Collins. "Rather, the multitude of actions undertaken after an acquaintance has been made should be the primary focus. No one can deny that her ladyship made a most excellent decision in choosing to install Mr. Collins as her parson. However, I say with no small amount of pride that I made a far better decision in selecting him as my husband."

"Certainly, a woman's husband is a man of no small influence in her life," said Lady Catherine, "yet of far greater influence is a man who has been placed in such a position as that of a clergyman who must attend to the spiritual well-being of his flock."

While Kitty watched this exchange with wide eyes, Elizabeth could scarcely stand to witness it at all. The two women acted as two dogs fighting over a delectable bone—and Mr. Collins, unbelievable as it was, held the position of the much-desired bone.

Casting her gaze about in an effort to either distract the two women or distract herself, Elizabeth noticed Mr. Darcy gazing at her with obvious amusement in his eyes.

"Mr. Darcy," said Elizabeth, glad to have caught someone's attention, "I noticed you were already acquainted with the Collinses. Had you met them previously in London?"

"I have encountered them at Rosings," said he. "As a result, I am accustomed to being in company with them and my aunt."

Elizabeth felt her lip twitch in a barely suppressed smile. Though he had not said it outright, she knew he meant that he was accustomed to Mr. and Mrs. Collins's silliness.

Even as Elizabeth and Mr. Darcy talked, the tug-of-war continued. Still, Elizabeth believed she might as well attempt to ignore it. Looking pointedly at Mr. Darcy, she said: "While I am no great musician, I should like to avail myself of the pianoforte. I wonder whether you would be interested in trying your skills as a page-turner."

"I should like to practice those skills, as it has been some time since they were exercised," said Mr. Darcy lightly.

Elizabeth and Mr. Darcy moved to the pianoforte, whereupon Elizabeth immediately set to playing. There was a brief pause in the other conversation in the room before it resumed. Once it had, Elizabeth grimaced and murmured to Mr. Darcy: "Do they always behave in this fashion when in company together?"

"I should never have expected them to do so," said he quietly, "but unfortunately, an interaction of this sort is not uncommon."

A few moments later, Mr. Darcy said in quiet tones: "I will note, however, that Collins used to be much more long-winded before he married. Now, he has learned the art of keeping his mouth closed whenever his wife and my aunt are in a room together."

Elizabeth could not hold back her smile. "Perhaps marriage has made my cousin wise indeed."

"I suppose marriage can have a profound effect on many people."

Elizabeth glanced at her sister, who was concentrating on her needlework while wearing a closed-off expression.

With a trace of sadness, Elizabeth said: "I only wish marriage could change all men for the better."

Mr. Darcy lifted his arm slightly, as if he intended to touch her arm with his fingertips. Elizabeth felt the breath catch in her throat, but then he withdrew his hand from where it hovered nearby and used it to slowly turn the page of music. As Elizabeth continued to pay, she felt an inexplicable sense of loss.

Shortly thereafter, Mrs. Collins chose to address her. "This song is a rather melancholy one. Miss Elizabeth, I believe we would all be much better off if you played something livelier."

"I must disagree," said Lady Catherine. "I believe that Miss Elizabeth has chosen just the proper sort of song."

"Perhaps the song might be appropriate for a large group, but it is not well-suited for the present company."

Elizabeth did not wholly succeed in cutting off her amused chuckle as she covered her mouth with her shoulder, all while trying not to cease playing the pianoforte.

Mr. Darcy must have heard her muffled noise, as he looked intently at her. She did not even bother hiding the grin that attached itself to her mouth as she met his eyes.

Slowly, Mr. Darcy smiled, and she was surprised by how warm his smile was. Then she heard a low sound not unlike a chuckle, and her mirth only grew all the more.

CHAPTER IX

An hour before his aunt's dinner party was to begin, Darcy sat in the study of his aunt's townhouse with Henry. Neither of their faces bore smiles or even the barest hint of warm brotherhood.

After briefly tipping back his glass of port, Henry frowned as he realized the glass was empty. Shaking it in irritation, he said: "Fitz, please do remind me again why I must be forced to suffer through my aunt's misguided efforts to instill culture and sophistication in Miss Bennet."

"You should need no reminder that *Miss Bennet* is to one day become your wife," said Darcy, barely able to force back his frustration enough to make a civil reply.

"I hardly think such a farce as this deserves any of my consideration. The guest list is so saturated with members of our two families as to make the whole sodden affair as enthusiasm-engendering as a wet handkerchief."

Sighing, Darcy said: "You know the guests were selected primarily due to their intimacy with our families."

Indeed, the list of invitees was composed of relatives and close friends, with guests including the two male Darcys, Miss Elizabeth and Miss Kitty, Mr. and Mrs. Gardiner, Mr. Bingley, and Mr. and Mrs. Livingston. The remainder of the guest list was comprised of the earl and his wife as well as his oldest son and the effervescent Colonel Fitzwilliam. No doubt that was one of the reasons for Henry's distaste, as his uncle would tolerate no unseemly behavior in his relatives.

"There shall certainly be no new comely young women at this unfortunate gathering," said Henry, revealing another reason for his reluctance to participate in the dinner party. "However can I be expected to entertain myself without fresh blood to tease my senses?"

Darcy grimaced. "Henry, there is a subject I have intended to broach with you, and I might as well do so now. I believe the temptations of London have proven themselves to be too much for you to avoid—"

"Why should I want to avoid them?" asked Henry with a lift of his brow.

"—and we all would be better served should you extend an invitation to Haskett Hall to Miss Bennet and her two sisters."

"Why not broaden the invitation to include all four of her sisters and her parents besides?" asked Henry, waving a hand around in the air as he sneered at his brother. "In fact, mayhap it would be best if all of Hertfordshire should choose to descend upon my beloved home with nary a thought as to the effect such an intrusion would have on my well-being."

"I should never go so far as to call Haskett Hall beloved by you," said Darcy, pinning his brother with a look. "A more apt term would be 'neglected.' I suspect it has been some time since last you checked on the status of your estate. While I have been doing what I can to keep your inheritance from being carried off by the wind, there are some decisions that only the estate's owner can make. Though you may not deserve the title, you *are* the master of Haskett Hall."

Henry took a few moments to pour himself some more port before responding. "I am not inclined to leave London."

"That may be, but I fear I must insist. You are an engaged man, and you would do better to act as one. Leaving London and its vices could only do you well."

Though Darcy half-expected to hear continued protests, Henry instead studied Darcy over his brimming glass of wine. "You will not be dissuaded?"

"I will not."

"Even if I remind you of the scandal involved in having an engaged couple residing in the same house?"

"The engagement is not public knowledge, and I fear you will do worse damage if you continue in London as you have been."

"Then I suppose I can do nothing but acquiesce," said Henry with a sigh, "as I shall receive no rest otherwise."

Darcy merely nodded in response, not wishing to say anything that might cause his brother to retract his agreement. Though suspicious of the ease with which Henry had conceded, Darcy turned his mind to other matters.

After Lady Catherine had reached the end of her lecture on how to properly host such an intimate affair, she had commanded a pair of maids to assist Elizabeth and her two sisters in readying themselves for the evening. Though Elizabeth would have been much more comfortable undergoing the necessary preparations at the Gardiners' home on Gracechurch Street, she had known that there would be no gainsaying Lady Catherine when the forceful suggestion had been made the previous day for Elizabeth and Kitty to be tended to at Lady Catherine's townhouse.

Unfortunately, Elizabeth's maid had been efficient in assisting with dressing her and styling her hair, which meant Elizabeth found herself with an excess of free time. Rather than allow herself to be ensnared by Lady Catherine once more, she determined to occupy part of her time with reading. While on her way to select a book for this purpose, she had paused at the sound of the two Darcy brothers speaking and had, unscrupulously, eavesdropped on their conversation.

She had listened with approval to Mr. Darcy's efforts to persuade his brother of the necessity of leaving London, and once the man had succeeded, she hurried away, not wishing to be caught spying on them.

"That man," said she to herself, her irritation toward Henry Darcy simmering within her, "has all the maturity of a boy of three, but perhaps time shall cure that ill. I can only hope that removing him from London shall be as effective at forcing restraint as removing a plate of sweetmeats from the reach of a child."

But even as she wished to scold Henry Darcy, she wished to thank his brother. Her gratitude toward Mr. Darcy felt warm in her breast, for she appreciated the realization that he was just as desirous as she was for the union between his brother and her sister to be a happy one.

Elizabeth thus found herself to be in a better mood than was typical of late when she was introduced a short while later to the earl, his wife, and his two sons. She felt certain her father, had he been present, would have been disappointed in the earl's character, for though the man seemed appropriately somber, an unmistakable fatigue marked his eyes, and he remained less than inclined to speak.

The earl's wife appeared to be mild in temperament, with a kindness evident despite the reserved nature of her smiles. In contrast, the earl's oldest son appeared to be haughty and withdrawn. The family was redeemed by the youngest son, however, a pleasant young man named Colonel Fitzwilliam who made himself an immediate favorite of Elizabeth's with his charm and easy smile. That he spoke pleasantly with the Gardiners only raised him in her regard, though she took note that even Mr. Darcy ventured to speak with her aunt and uncle directly.

"I believe everyone is present now," said Lady Catherine in satisfaction, directing her words to Jane, Elizabeth, and Kitty, the three of whom she had encouraged to remain near her. "It is a rather good number for a first undertaking, is it not?"

Jane murmured a reply, as did Kitty a moment later, but Elizabeth refrained from saying anything at all, fearing her response might be impertinent indeed.

Once the party had gathered around the table, Elizabeth kept a close eye on Henry Darcy. Lady Catherine had maneuvered the guests so that the young man sat near Jane, but he seemed more interested in his wine glass than conversation with his fiancée.

"Do you find the food to your liking?" asked Mr. Darcy, who sat across from Elizabeth.

She looked down and realized she had been suspending a forkful of food in midair for what might have been a full minute as she contemplated the relationship between her sister and Mr. Henry Darcy. She flushed and gave Mr. Darcy a wan smile. "The food is splendid, thank you. Lady Catherine's table shall always be a fine one, I am certain."

"I suppose your thoughts lay elsewhere, then," said he quietly.

"Indeed, they do," replied she. In the middle of such a gathering, neither one of them could say more, but she thought they understood one another's meaning well enough.

Rallying her thoughts, she proceeded to carry on her conversation with Mr. Darcy, changing the subject to a more pleasant one.

While she enjoyed speaking to Mr. Darcy, she grew worried as she noticed his brother's frequent requests for servants to refill his glass. The young man's cheeks began to take on a red hue as he eschewed the food placed before him in favor of more wine. She feared something ill would come of his heavy drinking. Her fears soon became realized.

The trouble began when Lady Catherine made a broad gesture at the table and told Jane: "You can see how the shine of the silverware adds a distinctly elegant air to even a small dinner party such as this. That is why you must always check everything that the servants do. You cannot simply trust them to obey the directive to polish the cutlery until it shines, for most servants are lazy and hope they can accomplish any assignments with minimal effort. Why, I once had a servant who had been at Rosings for more than ten years—"

"Enough, your ladyship," barked Henry Darcy, waving a sluggish hand in the air. "Any daft bird with half a brain could serve as a host, and worrying about whether your spoons shine should be the least of a person's concerns. While my fiancée may not be the brightest girl in London, even she can accomplish hosting a dinner party without trouble if she is given a few capable servants to aid her."

"How dare you speak such slander against my sister?" cried Elizabeth in unmitigated outrage. "Jane may be more reserved than the witless women with whom you are accustomed to speaking, but nobody in possession of a brain could say she lacks one."

Kitty gasped, and Jane pleaded quietly but urgently: "*Lizzy*!"

"I dare say you have not been acquainted with me long enough to know what sort of women typically draw my eye," said Henry Darcy, sneering at Elizabeth. "Furthermore, I think your estimation of your sister is too great."

"*Henry*," said his brother sharply, attempting to quell him.

"I speak only the truth!" cried the man. "Can you claim to have ever participated in intelligent conversation with Miss Bennet?"

"Mr. Henry Darcy," said Kitty suddenly, "even if you are related to an earl, you cannot treat one of my sisters in such an abominable fashion. You would do well to watch your words."

Henry Darcy glanced at her, no doubt surprised by her forcefulness.

"Miss Kitty is quite right," said Colonel Fitzwilliam. "I believe you are not taking enough care with the words exiting your mouth. Perhaps you should refrain from drinking anything further this evening."

Henry Darcy laughed and took a pointed gulp of wine. "We are all close here, are we not? This dinner party was meant to be an intimate affair—friends and family and all that. We might as well be honest with one another. Jane Bennet may be a beauty, but in truth, she is a terrible bore."

"The *truth* is that you have had too much to drink, Henry," said the earl, having stirred himself from his lethargy to address the inappropriate behavior of his nephew. "I would suggest you close your mouth before you say anything more damaging than you already have."

Elizabeth did not miss the earl's troubled glance at Mr. Gardiner. Her uncle's face held a grimness that she had never seen there before.

Henry Darcy, despite his intoxication, seemed to notice the reason for his uncle's concern, and he waved his hand vaguely in the air.

"You need not worry about the possibility of my offending her family," said he. "After all, they need one of their daughters to marry a Darcy."

Though the Bennets could have benefited from a marital connection with someone of good fortune, they did not *require* it, and Elizabeth could not countenance such blatant impropriety. Her uncle could not do so either.

"Mr. Henry Darcy," began Mr. Gardiner in a voice that shook with anger, only to cease speaking as Lady Catherine shoved her chair backward and shot to her feet.

She stepped toward her nephew and then slapped him, the sound of the impact ringing out in the room. The young man stared at her, his jaw slackened with shock.

"Since long before you were born," said her ladyship stiffly, "the Darcy name has been synonymous with good breeding. What you have displayed here tonight is nothing of the sort. I have never been more ashamed of one of my relations than I am right now.

"Jane Bennet is a graceful, kind-hearted, and *intelligent* girl who shall do you credit as a wife. I have only been trying to ease her way in society so that her transition shall be easier for her to handle, for I know there are those who will believe her to be nothing more than a chaser of prestige. Even without my guidance, however, I do not believe she could ever do anything that would bring shame to your family.

"Henry, I know you have been taught the importance of propriety, but at present, *you* seem to be the one in need of training."

Lady Catherine's words, though by no means loud, filled the dining hall no less impressively than the resonance of a gunshot would have. In those brief moments while the dinner party participants held their breaths and waited for Henry Darcy's response, the passage of a mouse would have seemed deafening.

Henry Darcy's eyes left Lady Catherine's face to travel the room. The anger Elizabeth felt was mirrored on the faces of the Gardiners and Kitty, and Henry's relations and the Livingstons seemed to be experiencing varying degrees of disgust and disappointment. Even Mr. Bingley's expression was tight with anger.

Henry Darcy must have realized he had no friends at that table, for the ruddiness of his face paled slightly.

His voice dark but quiet, Mr. Gardiner said: "I would suggest that you proffer an apology to my niece and improve your behavior, or else I, in her father's place, will be forced to do something no gentleman ever hopes to be called to do."

Elizabeth and Kitty exchanged a wide-eyed look. Though Elizabeth could not even begin to describe the magnitude of her offense at Henry Darcy's words that evening, she had not thought the insults to be so outrageous as to lead her uncle to consider calling the man out.

Still, after considering the situation briefly, she supposed that everything had been leading up to this. How could Jane be expected to marry someone so utterly lacking in not just decorum, but basic morality? His treatment of Jane was repulsive, and though Elizabeth had not addressed her concerns with Mr. Gardiner, she supposed he had not been blind to the situation between Henry Darcy and Jane.

Biting her lip, she could not help but wonder how Mr. Darcy had taken the veiled threat to his brother. She glanced at him and saw, to her surprise, the elder Darcy giving Henry a stony look.

Elizabeth looked at Jane, then, worried about how the current situation had affected her.

Jane was staring down at her lap, so it was difficult to see her face, but Elizabeth thought her countenance seemed pale. At her side, Mrs. Livingston whispered something into Jane's ear which only produced a slight jerk of Jane's head in response.

"Very well," said Henry Darcy suddenly. "I know when I am beaten."

With obvious distaste, the young man gave a slight bow of his head to Jane and said stiffly: "I apologize for my words, Miss Bennet."

Jane murmured something in response, and though it seemed unlikely even Henry Darcy understood what she said, he turned to look at the Gardiners. "I would also like to extend my apologies to Miss Bennet's family. I fear I have had too much to drink."

Mr. and Mrs. Gardiner gave curt nods, both apparently unable to conjure up speech, and after they had done so, Henry Darcy excused himself from the table.

Elizabeth might have expected an easing of tensions once the young man had left the room, but the occupants of the room could not be calmed by such a begrudging apology. The Gardiners certainly did not seem appeased by Henry Darcy's words; instead, they looked both troubled and angry. Even Lady Catherine's face held all the expectant tension of a bull readying itself to charge at an unsuspecting target.

Elizabeth and the other attendees of the dinner party eventually returned to eating their meal, but the food tasted like ash on Elizabeth's tongue. She scarcely knew what she had put in her mouth by the time she stood from the table. Fortunately, Lady Catherine did not appear to expect her guests to shower her with compliments, for she dismissed everyone early, claiming an indisposition. In other circumstances, such a dismissal might have been considered rude, but that evening, everyone appeared to feel relieved for the opportunity to return to calmer surroundings.

Elizabeth moved to speak to Jane briefly before leaving, wanting to know if she would be well despite Henry Darcy's words, but Mrs. Livingston caught Jane's attention first, inundating her with furious whispers.

Suppressing her aggravation, Elizabeth began to follow the Gardiners as they moved to depart, but before she had exited the townhouse, Mr. Darcy pulled her aside.

"Miss Bennet," said he, speaking quietly, "I wish to apologize for my brother's behavior."

Elizabeth's lip twitched, and she felt her anger at Henry Darcy rise once more. "The only one who needs to apologize at present is your brother himself."

"Nevertheless," said Mr. Darcy, "I apologize sincerely. Furthermore, I would like to immediately extend an invitation for you and your two sisters to come to Haskett Hall in Leicestershire. I know you must not wish to enter my brother's home at present, but I believe his departure from London to be necessary, and I would ask that you consider the notion.

"Since my brother is engaged to your sister, it would do them both well to spend some time together in advance of being married. Furthermore, your sister must wish to see the estate of which she will be the future mistress. My aunt has agreed to serve as a chaperone, so your father and Mr. Gardiner need not worry about anything untoward. I know these circumstances are less than ideal, but I would encourage you to consider accepting."

Before that evening, Elizabeth would have been surprised to learn that Lady Catherine had agreed to anything so altruistic as leaving London to serve as a chaperone to three young women. Now, however, she harbored a new respect for the woman, and her unkind thoughts had greatly diminished.

"I will consider the invitation," said Elizabeth a few moments later, "and I will speak to my uncle about it before writing to my father for permission. I suspect Jane shall agree to go, but I would like to take a little time before we accept."

"Of course," said Mr. Darcy, bowing his head. "I would expect you to discuss the invitation with your family."

She gave him a brief grateful smile and pressed his arm, and then she was gone.

Chapter X

In light of Henry Darcy's recent actions, Mr. Gardiner naturally expressed some reservations about the notion of Jane traveling to Haskett Hall, but a discussion with his wife and Elizabeth soon convinced him that the idea held merit, and he agreed to seek Mr. Bennet's permission.

Before Elizabeth wrote him, however, she called upon Jane at Lady Catherine's townhouse in order to determine her sister's feelings on the subject. Lady Catherine seemed less inclined to speak than normal, her sober mood no doubt reflective of the previous evening's catastrophic end, so Elizabeth found herself able to broach the topic of a trip much sooner than she had hoped.

"Mr. Darcy and his brother have extended an invitation for us to come to Haskett Hall, Jane," said Elizabeth, watching to see her sister's reaction.

Jane remained unreadable, but Lady Catherine replied in her stead. "I have already discussed the issue with Miss Bennet, and she has agreed to accept the offer. While I ordinarily would not countenance the notion of a young woman traveling with her two sisters so that they might stay at her fiancé's estate, I have already agreed to serve as your chaperone, so no one need fear for your well-being. Furthermore, since the engagement has not been made public, we need not worry about any idle tongues creating trouble concerning the issue of an engaged couple staying in the same house together. I believe it to be a wholly necessary evil in this instance. I am more than aware of the beneficial effect that a departure from London shall have on my unruly nephew, and I can only praise any venture that accomplishes it."

Despite the ever-present confidence she projected, Lady Catherine appeared to be avoiding looking directly at Elizabeth. Though there had been times when Elizabeth had unkindly wondered whether her ladyship ever experienced such self-deriding feelings as shame, she realized that the woman refused to let her pride in her family blind her to Mr. Henry Darcy's shortcomings. Even Lady Catherine could become embarrassed.

Smiling to herself, glad that her sister would have another ally, Elizabeth said: "Then I suppose I shall ask my father for permission on behalf of all three of us."

Jane dipped her head in response and said softly: "Thank you, Lizzy."

Though the response could not be called enthusiastic, Elizabeth supposed she would have to accept it.

After gaining Jane's approval, Elizabeth wrote to her father. She had agreed with the Gardiners that it would not be appropriate to detail the events of the dinner party in a letter, and her uncle advised that he intended to have a long discussion with Mr. Bennet the next time they met in person to apprise him of the expression of Henry Darcy's volatility.

Elizabeth half-expected her mother to respond to her letter in her father's stead, as Mr. Bennet could rarely be bothered to write at all, but the man actually managed to send a few lines, offering his begrudging approval for Elizabeth, Jane, and Kitty to travel to Haskett Hall and imparting a few witticisms.

After reading her father's letter, Elizabeth wasted no time in giving Mr. Darcy the news.

"I am glad to hear that you will all be coming," said Mr. Darcy quietly. "My sister has been at Pemberley with her companion, Mrs. Annesley, and I have requested that they join us at Haskett Hall. I suspect you shall quickly befriend Georgiana, if I know anything about your character."

"I should like that," said Elizabeth with a smile. "However, I am surprised that you believe you are already familiar with my character despite the short length of our acquaintance. Should I be offended that my actions are so easy to predict?"

"Certainly not," said Mr. Darcy warmly. "My opinions concerning your character are merely the result of some study."

It was only later that Elizabeth thought to wonder at the fact that Mr. Darcy considered her to be worthy of studying at all.

The day before Elizabeth departed London found her seated in Lady Catherine's drawing-room with Jane, Kitty, and her ladyship. After making a few failed attempts to draw Jane away from Lady Catherine, Elizabeth finally surrendered and turned her attention to a volume of poetry. When Caroline Livingston arrived, Elizabeth felt a flicker of envy as the woman pulled Jane aside under the pretense of encouraging Jane to stretch her legs.

The two murmured together across the room before Mrs. Livingston released Jane. Surprisingly, however, Mrs. Livingston looked over at Elizabeth and said: "Miss Eliza Bennet, I wonder whether you might take a turn about the room with me."

Though uncertain of the reason for Mrs. Livingston's request, Elizabeth agreed to join her, and the two slowly walked toward the side of the room opposite from Jane, Kitty, and Lady Catherine.

When Mrs. Livingston paused under the pretense of examining a decorative bust, Elizabeth said quietly: "I suppose there is a reason you wished to speak with me privately." She had expected that a confrontation with the other woman would be forthcoming at some point, and she supposed it might as well occur before they parted ways.

"Certainly, there is," said Mrs. Livingston with a tight smile. "I wished to speak with you about Jane before you left London."

Though she felt a flash of protectiveness toward her dear sister, Elizabeth held her tongue and waited for Mrs. Livingston's elucidation.

"I suspect you are aware of Henry Darcy's proclivities by this point," said Mrs. Livingston in a low voice, "so I shall not detail the reasons for concern on that front. I have been attempting to lighten your sister's spirits and provide some comfort, but I fear my efforts have not been as effective as I would like."

Elizabeth felt her jaw slacken as Mrs. Livingston's words washed over her. "What?"

"You seem stunned," said Mrs. Livingston with dark amusement as she looked upon Elizabeth. "I suppose it is not surprising to find that your opinion of me is so low. No doubt you believe I have been attempting to keep your sister to myself."

Elizabeth began to protest, but Mrs. Livingston waved her off. "It does not signify. Perhaps my motives were not entirely selfless when I began to seek out your sister's company, but I have come to view her as a friend."

"I do not understand your meaning—"

"Because we cannot speak much longer without garnering unwanted attention, I shall tell you directly why I wished to speak with you. To put it bluntly, I believe my brother is in love with your sister. Unfortunately, since your sister is already engaged, I cannot foster a relationship between them. Still, I decided I could at least attempt to comfort Jane and ease her way. Such a thing is a comfort to Charles as well. I know her depression has affected him deeply."

Elizabeth felt her brow furrowing as she attempted to make sense of this version of Mrs. Livingston, which was different from the more villainous one she had drawn up in her head. "I might have thought you would want your brother to make a better match than my sister."

"Perhaps there was a time when I would not have been overly concerned about my brother's personal feelings. However, when my sister, Louisa, passed away a few years ago, I was utterly devastated by the loss, and Charles proved himself to be a pillar of unexpected strength and comfort. When my spirits finally rallied, I resolved to repay him in some way, and helping the woman he loves seems to be as good a method as any."

Though not surprised to hear that Charles Bingley loved Jane based on what she had seen, Elizabeth was rather curious as to how it came about. After all, the image Jane had been presenting since Elizabeth's arrival in London had been a rather lifeless one. "Are you certain his feelings are not pity or sympathy instead?"

Mrs. Livingston frowned, and she took a moment to respond. "I suppose you wonder about the reason for his feelings given how reserved your sister has shown herself to be. Her demeanor was different when she first arrived in London—pleasant and more hopeful for her future than she is now. My brother does not typically take long to fall in love, but he tends to just as quickly fall out of it. With your sister, however, the more she withdrew, the deeper he fell. When I realized his feelings were sincere and not temporary, I resolved to befriend her and serve as a source of solace.

"Unfortunately, I cannot assist Jane any longer since she will be leaving for Haskett Hall, but I will not hesitate to part with her since you shall be at her side. Still, I do feel it prudent to warn you that your sister needs to become accustomed to the society with which Mr. Henry Darcy surrounds himself. Avoiding it is pointless, as his society shall be part of her future once she marries him. Short of breaking off the engagement, there is nothing she can do."

Feeling a sense of powerlessness alongside her general unhappiness, Elizabeth could only nod. There was nothing else to be done.

"Besides," said Mrs. Livingston, "there are other things that may bring Jane happiness. For instance, I am even now with child."

"Then I must congratulate you," said Elizabeth with a gentle smile. "You must be very happy."

"I am," said Mrs. Livingston. She paused and then spoke again. "I believe your sister will make an excellent mother one day."

It was true that Jane would be the most excellent of mothers, though her children would be spoiled beyond belief. Perhaps it was also true that Jane would be able to one day find her own slice of happiness even in such discouraging circumstances.

CHAPTER XI

The carriage ride to Haskett Hall was a somber affair. Jane spoke only when addressed, and Lady Catherine seemed ill-inclined to voice anything other than complaints about the weather, the bumpiness of their travel, and the coach's cramped conditions. Elizabeth and Kitty briefly attempted some light conversation before surrendering to silence. At that moment, Elizabeth envied the Darcys and Mr. Bingley, as they were able to ride their horses and avoid the stifling air of the carriage.

When the first day of travel finally ended, Elizabeth stepped out of the carriage with a profound sense of relief. One might have thought they were part of a funeral procession judging by their somber countenances.

On the second day of travel, Elizabeth resolved to transform the atmosphere of the carriage into something less oppressive. When the others remained unresponsive, she tried to maintain a running monologue. Finally, when Elizabeth felt she could scarcely bear the tension any longer, Lady Catherine shook off the morose streak that had overcome her, and she began to carry on a conversation with Elizabeth before demonstrating her normal imperious nature once more.

"Much work awaits you at Haskett Hall," said Lady Catherine, looking at Jane suddenly. "Unfortunately, your husband-to-be takes more pride in his looks than in the estate left to him by his father. Nonetheless, I am confident that, in time, you shall be able to effect a transformation in both man and estate. It shall merely take a steady hand and persistence. I believe you are more than capable, Miss Bennet, so you need not be concerned in your ability to complete the task."

Jane murmured her gratitude for Lady Catherine's compliment, and Elizabeth wondered at Lady Catherine's comments about Haskett Hall. Was the estate's condition truly so terrible?

She at last found the occasion to enlighten herself when Mr. Darcy tapped on the window and advised Elizabeth that they were approaching the estate. Not caring about the inelegance of their actions, Elizabeth and Kitty both crowded around one of the windows and peered out to observe the countryside. Jane remained where she was, looking out the other window to view as much as she could without changing position.

As they traveled, the land took on a decidedly wild appearance. But it was not the pleasurable wild such as might be found in a field of wildflowers; rather, the unkempt look of the area was formed by the snarls of brambles and choking weeds, products of neglect rather than a love for the bounty of the earth.

Elizabeth glanced at Mr. Darcy, who rode nearby. His expression seemed grim, but when he saw her looking at him, he gave a nod of the head and a tight smile.

"I suppose the estate's master has been away for too long," murmured he before he pulled his horse back to speak with Henry Darcy.

"Do you think Mr. Darcy intends to castigate his brother?" asked Kitty quietly.

"I should not be surprised," said Elizabeth. Had Lady Catherine not been present, Elizabeth might have said more, but she thought it wise to refrain from commenting further.

Elizabeth did not learn whether Mr. Darcy reprimanded his brother, but she did soon hear Lady Catherine take on the task once the gentleman had dismounted and the ladies had exited the carriage.

"Had I not known the truth, I might have thought your father died thirty years ago based on the state of this place," said Lady Catherine, stabbing at the ground with her cane. "Henry, have you no pride in what has been bequeathed upon you?"

"The appearance of the grounds does not signify," said the young man, unintimidated by his aunt. "The fields are in acceptable enough shape."

"Your neighbors must think you as wild and unbridled as a stallion," cried Lady Catherine. "Would that you were born as a horse rather than as my nephew!" With that, she marched ahead, the stiffness of her back and the tightness of her grip on her cane serving as signs of her displeasure.

"That went well," said Henry Darcy sarcastically. He then looked at his guests and made a sweeping gesture. "Welcome home."

Then, before anybody else could say a word, he advanced forward and into the house.

Elizabeth exchanged a glance with Kitty, but neither was willing to say anything in their present company, so they kept their thoughts to themselves.

Mr. Darcy, though his face had been beset by storm clouds, soon took on the office of introducing the housekeeper. Mrs. Williamson was a kind yet flustered older woman. Elizabeth suspected her to be unaccustomed to having guests, though the woman's agitation might have been due to the sight of Lady Catherine's imperious glare. Though the look had not been directed against Mrs. Williamson, it could only produce discomfort in anyone who beheld it.

A more interesting character study came in the person of the estate's steward. When their eyes met, Mr. Darcy and Mr. Wickham exchanged a cold murmured greeting. Mr. Bingley and Lady Catherine revealed themselves as having been previously acquainted with the man, whose father had apparently been a favorite of the late Mr. Darcy, but Mr. Darcy performed the office of introducing Mr. Wickham to the three Bennet sisters. His words, however, were stilted and reluctant, a byproduct of necessity rather than desire.

Unaffected by the lack of effort put forth, Mr. Wickham smiled and said with a slight bow: "It is a pleasure to make the acquaintance of three such charming young women."

"The pleasure is ours," returned Elizabeth.

From Mr. Wickham's continuing smile and focused look, Elizabeth suspected he felt inclined to speak further with her and her sisters, but Mr. Darcy pulled him aside along with Mr. Bingley for some brief discussion. She watched them for a few moments and wondered at Mr. Wickham's behavior, for she felt he seemed rather forward for a man employed as a steward.

Mrs. Williamson took the opportunity to conduct a brief tour for the three Bennets. Lady Catherine, who was already familiar with the residence, excused herself.

Though larger than Longbourn, Haskett Hall did not impart the sense of ease and comfort that Longbourn did. The furnishings were dated, and there was a sterility to the place that made it feel as if nobody lived there. That was to say nothing against Mrs. Williamson, for she had tended to the place and kept it clean. Rather, the fault could only be attributed to the estate's master. Henry Darcy obviously did not spend much of his time at his estate.

The housekeeper showed Jane to a room of her own, but she showed Elizabeth and Kitty to a room that they would share. Though the age of the furniture inside bore further evidence of the master's lack of care, its cleanliness further reflected the fact that the housekeeper bore no fault in the state of the house.

"I am sorry that I cannot better accommodate you," said Mrs. Williamson, "but not all of the rooms are suited for living in at present. I fear I was not given sufficient notice of your coming."

Elizabeth smiled at her. "You need not be concerned. As there are five Bennet daughters living at an estate with a modest income, we are no strangers to sharing rooms. In truth, I welcome the opportunity to be so close with one of my sisters, particularly when I find myself in new surroundings."

"You are quite the delight," said Mrs. Williamson warmly. "If Miss Bennet proves herself to be only half as pleasant as you, then I am certain I will count myself to be fortunate indeed."

"Then you may call yourself fortunate even now, for Jane is the best woman you shall ever meet. You will never hear a cross word from her."

"Is that so?" asked Mrs. Williamson.

"It is indeed," said Kitty. "Jane never says anything unkind to anybody."

"Well, I dare say this old estate will be glad indeed to have a proper mistress tending to her," said Mrs. Williamson. She then frowned and patted her gray hair absently. "I suppose it scarcely bears mentioning, but I would like to, ah, remind you that it is not a good idea to roam outside your room late at night."

"Are their spirits who would leap at us?" asked Kitty eagerly.

"No, no, nothing of the sort," said the housekeeper. "It is simply good practice, you know. Please promise me you will abide by this old lady's wishes."

"Certainly, we have no intention to wander the house at night," said Elizabeth. The request seemed a rather odd one, but there could be no harm in offering reassurance that they would abide by it.

Mrs. Williamson dipped her head. "I am glad to hear it. Quite glad."

Darcy could sometimes barely restrain himself from throttling his brother. Henry had no sense of propriety or dignity, merely a pride in himself as a man. Embarrassment was an utterly foreign concept to him, as Darcy was soon reminded.

After Darcy had changed out of his traveling garments, he had gone to find his brother. When Henry could not be located in the drawing-room or the study, Darcy had knocked on the door to Henry's chambers.

No reply had come, but Darcy had thought he heard a hushed voice, so he had opened the door with a sense of infuriated righteousness, launching into his reprimand and stepping into the room before even settling his eyes on his brother:

"Henry, I cannot—"

Darcy had then quickly backed out of the room and slammed the door, mortified.

He took a moment to collect himself, and as his anger rose, he cracked open the door and growled through the opening: "Henry, meet me in the study *posthaste*."

His scowl darkened further when he heard a distinctly feminine giggle, but he closed the door instead of lingering. Then he stalked away, taking himself to the study to await his brother's arrival.

Some minutes later, Henry entered the room, sloppily dressed and dripping with amusement.

"The fact that I am required to conduct such a lecture as this is almost beyond my capacity to comprehend, so stunned am I by the abhorrently uncaring nature of your actions. With your fiancée in residence, you would stoop to meet with your mistress on the very day of your arrival home?"

"Is there a better time to meet with her then?" asked Henry as he dropped into a chair. "Stop being such a bore, Darcy."

"Perhaps the engagement that binds you is not one of your own making, but you cannot place the blame at Miss Bennet's feet. She deserves more consideration than you have given her."

Since this reprimand only rewarded Darcy with an eye roll and a dismissive wave, he decided to attempt a different form of persuasion. "Need I remind you that Georgiana will be joining us soon? If you do not want her to glimpse your utter disdain for morality, then you would do well to eschew the sort of behavior that shall make it more than obvious that you are not quite the brother whom she believes you to be."

Henry's bored expression transformed into a sober one. "You need not be concerned on that front, Fitz. I shall ensure that not even the slightest chance shall exist that Georgie shall happen upon my light o' love."

Darcy's lip twitched. "Meaning?"

"Meaning the girl shall be gone before Georgie arrives."

"Good," said Darcy. Though he wished to argue for the girl's immediate removal, he knew Henry would not heed his wishes or commands. At least Henry's mistress would not be staying for long. "I must say I am surprised that you would have ventured to be so bold with our aunt in residence."

"I shall never let that old bird affect what I do."

Shaking his head, Darcy could only acknowledge to himself that it was nothing more than the truth. Henry had never been one to even listen to what Lady Catherine said, much less obey her whims or commands in any way.

"Very well," said Darcy. "Then there is another matter I wish to discuss with you. When are you going to replace your steward?"

Henry's snort showed his opinion of that. "Wickham does well enough. I see no need to replace him."

The heat rose in Darcy's face. As Wickham did nothing that required any sort of effort, he certainly did not apply himself to any of his duties as steward. The man served as steward in name only. The bulk of the work was performed by Darcy and his own steward, the ever-capable Mr. Barnes.

But as birds resorted unto their like, so did Henry and Wickham enjoy spending time together exploring their vices. Wickham's laziness and immorality formed the primary reasons for Darcy's dislike of him, though many others praised Wickham as being genial and well-mannered.

"He is a bad man and a worse influence," said Darcy, restraining himself from labeling Wickham with the sort of colorful language that the man rightly deserved.

"You simply have no capacity for fun."

"Henry," said Darcy, running a hand through his hair as he felt his exasperation grow, "you shall be married ere long, and you need to exert yourself to become something that at least *resembles* a gentleman. Jane Bennet does not deserve what is to come to her."

"She certainly does not deserve the Darcy money," muttered Henry.

"What money?" growled Darcy. "My efforts and the efforts of Mr. Barnes are all that keep Haskett Hall from collapsing upon itself. If you ruin Jane Bennet—"

"If I ruin Jane Bennet, then what? Why does it concern you, Darcy?" asked Henry, a flash of fire in his eyes as he jumped to his feet. "In the past, you have always been inclined to give me enough rope to hang myself as long as it does not reflect too negatively on your precious image."

"I have never understood your self-destructive tendencies, but I would like to remind you yet again that Miss Bennet has done nothing to be treated so callously."

"You are demonstrating yourself to have a lot of interest in the issue of Miss Bennet's well-being. One might wonder if you have your own hound in the hunt. Do not think that I have missed seeing how you look at Miss Elizabeth."

"That is ridiculous," said Darcy, his tone not as convincing as he would have liked.

"Oh, I rather think not," said Henry, settling back onto his chair with a satisfied smirk on his face. "I do believe that the clever Elizabeth Bennet has thawed the icy exterior of one Fitzwilliam Darcy. Of course, I am not surprised; I do find the young woman rather intriguing myself."

"Watch yourself," said Darcy darkly. "Stay away from Miss Elizabeth. I will not have you sullying her in some last misguided attempt at a dalliance before your marriage to her sister. Furthermore, you need to comport yourself in a fashion more befitting of the Darcy family honor."

"I have been watching the Darcy honor all this time, Fitz," said Henry sourly. "After all, I agreed to marry Jane Bennet, did I not? And I have stood by what I had said I would do."

"Keeping a woman such as *that one* here is not precisely standing by what you have claimed you will do."

"I am not married yet."

Darcy inhaled sharply. "Henry—"

"I am meeting my obligations, Fitz."

"You will have an obligation to be faithful to your wife."

"Again, I am not married yet," said Henry lightly.

"Please try to temper your behavior," said Darcy, knowing he might as well have been speaking to a wall made of stone. "And be certain to send your female *companion* away before Georgiana arrives."

After giving his brother a glare that was entirely ignored, Darcy left the room.

He could not help but fret over the issue of Georgiana's imminent arrival. Perhaps postponing her trip might be the wisest course to take, but he felt she could only benefit from the opportunity of meeting her future sisters. He and Henry had not provided her with the female companionship she must have craved, and her shy nature and position in society had only further distanced her from other people. The lighthearted natures of Miss Elizabeth and Miss Kitty would do much to increase her comfort in company.

But even as his hope for Georgiana grew, his hope for his brother weakened. The engagement still held, but it would no doubt be best for all involved if it could be dissolved. As the engagement had been divulged to only a select few, much of the damage could be contained if it were to be broken.

Still, Darcy recalled his dying father's pleas to maintain the engagement as both Darcy and Henry sat at his bedside. Though feverish and weak, the man had made fervent appeals for them to aid the Bennets and erase the debt he believed he owed.

Henry, with tears gleaming in his eyes, had promised the elder Mr. Darcy that he would do what he could to assist the Bennets.

It was that promise, made to a dying man, that chained Henry to marriage to Jane Bennet. For all his flaws, Henry had been close to his father. The man's death had had a profound impact on him.

Darcy did not doubt that Henry would do what he could to fulfill the promise that had been made. Yet Darcy feared that a marriage between Jane Bennet and Henry would ultimately do more harm than good.

CHAPTER XII

When Lady Catherine left the three Bennet sisters in the drawing-room while she went to speak with the housekeeper, Elizabeth seized the chance to talk to Jane. She could anticipate the results of their conversation, yet she felt it necessary to try to persuade her sister against a loveless marriage.

"Jane, I have been worried about your well-being," began Elizabeth. "I do not believe Mr. Henry Darcy to be the sort of man who could bring you any measure of happiness, and I believe the most prudent decision would be to break off the engagement entirely. I know you and your fiancé have no love for each other."

"Lizzy," said Jane gently, "you need not be concerned. I shall marry Mr. Henry Darcy without any regrets. I know it is not what either of us had imagined for my future when we were young girls, but I must do what I can to aid my family. Should something happen to Papa, then my mother and sisters shall need a place to stay. This marriage will bring our family security, and it shall only prove the advantage when it comes time for all of my sisters to wed."

Elizabeth, who feared that Mr. Henry Darcy would not escape the taint of scandal when he became a married man, could not share Jane's certainty in the advantageous nature of Jane's upcoming nuptials. "You know we care little for that, Jane."

"It is important to me," said Jane quietly.

"But you do not love the man," said Kitty. "How could you marry a man you do not love?"

The notion was not as foreign to Elizabeth as it was to Kitty, but Elizabeth nonetheless agreed with her in part. She did not see how Jane could flourish in a relationship that did not involve some small measure of love.

"I love my family," replied Jane, "and that brings me comfort enough."

Elizabeth looked down at Jane's hands, which rested in her lap. The young woman had clenched them together so tightly they had turned white. This sign of her sister's distress tore at Elizabeth's heart, and she knew she could no longer try to convince her.

"I wish to go outside for a walk," murmured Elizabeth, mostly speaking to Kitty.

Kitty moved to stand at the window and peer out of it. "Are you certain? I believe it may rain, Lizzy."

But Elizabeth felt stifled and trapped, and she could not remain in that room any longer with Jane, whom she viewed as a lamb waiting to be led to slaughter.

"I shall not be gone long," said she. "I find my legs in need of stretching."

Before Kitty could protest further, Elizabeth stood and left the room.

After gathering her outdoor accoutrements, Elizabeth hurried away from the house. She felt its presence at her back like some sort of weary beast, its windows cold eyes that bored into her back and caused a chill to pass over her. She pulled her wrap tighter, but it did little to instill her with any sense of warmth.

In truth, the weather was milder than one might have expected from a sunless sky, but an ill wind blew that removed any sense of comfort that might otherwise have been felt. Even as Elizabeth set out on her promenade to calm herself, she retained an inner sense that no good could come from her venture outdoors. Unfortunately, she was soon proven all too correct.

Her walk seemed uneventful at first. Though she felt challenged by the wildness of the estate's terrain, she refused to bow down to the vagaries of nature, and she forced her way through an overgrown field to reach what appeared to be a promising-looking path.

Unfortunately, at the edge of the field, she grew too complacent, and her lack of care led her to step into a hole in the ground. Her efforts to prevent her fall only served to twist her ankle, making her tumble even more painful.

Elizabeth sat up quickly and winced at the throbbing of her ankle. She reached out to touch it and cried out: "Ah!"

She sat there for a few minutes, trying to will the pain to diminish, but it refused to abate.

"I suppose I have only my own foolishness to thank for my misfortune," said she to herself. "I should not have attempted to navigate such a treacherous landscape as this."

Elizabeth wondered whether it was even worth standing at that point, yet she did not want to worry her sisters, and the grass and weeds had begun to prick at her legs through her skirts, so she forced herself upright and stumbled forward a few steps. The pain in her ankle seemed to strengthen with each movement, causing her to hobble forward with agonizing slowness.

And then it began to rain.

When Kitty heard the faint sound of raindrops, she flew to the window. The rain fell lightly at first, sprinkling the ground, but it soon began to fall in heavy sheets, obscuring Kitty's view of the outside. Kitty wondered whether Elizabeth would even be able to see the house if she attempted to return. Would Elizabeth become lost on the estate's weed-choked grounds?

As the minutes passed, Kitty's anxiety continued to rise. Finally, she turned to her eldest sister and said in a sort of plea: "Jane, Lizzy is outside in the rain."

Though Jane had seemed distracted, her sister's words were enough to cause a flicker of life to appear in her.

"Outside?" repeated she in confusion. She joined Kitty at the window and realized the reason for the girl's concern. "Lizzy is out in this weather? Do you know where she might have gone?"

"No," said Kitty, wringing her hands. "You know Lizzy and her walks. She does not always take the most obvious path."

"We should find Mr. Darcy," said Jane.

"I will do it," said Kitty, a firm note to her voice. Then she rushed outside the drawing-room.

In the hallway, Kitty stumbled into Henry Darcy, who seemed startled by her sudden appearance.

"Miss Kitty," said he with a raised brow, "might I ask why you appear to fit the role of one who is being trailed by ravenous wolves?"

"I am worried about my sister," snapped Kitty, in no mood for his levity. "If you have no desire to assist me, then I will find someone who will. Now, can you direct me to your brother or your aunt? I have no time to make idle chatter with you."

Henry Darcy blinked at her for a moment before he responded. "Well, I suppose Darcy might be in the study with Wickham."

Kitty gave him the barest hint of a curtsy before she rushed off to the study. After knocking and being granted entrance, she burst into the room.

Mr. Darcy's expression was one of annoyance and Mr. Wickham's one of boredom. Her appearance, however, caused their countenances to shift more to ones of surprise, any estate affairs they had been discussing forgotten.

"It is Lizzy," said Kitty, tense, anxious, and not entirely comprehensible. "She went outside to walk, but it—it is raining."

"Raining?" repeated Mr. Darcy, his brow furrowing.

"It is raining quite hard," said Kitty. "I worry she may not find her way back."

"You need not fear, Miss Kitty," said Mr. Wickham abruptly. "I will take my horse and go find her."

"No," said Mr. Darcy sharply, "*you* shall review your figures and these materials once more and try to find out the reason for that discrepancy we discussed. *I* shall go to find Miss Elizabeth."

Mr. Wickham appeared to be none-too-pleased by Mr. Darcy's command, but he merely nodded and turned his attention once more to the pile of papers sitting at the desk before him.

After leaving instructions with the housekeeper, Darcy aided a servant in saddling his horse, and then he set off across the grounds in a hunt for Elizabeth. Though he could scarcely believe the rain had grown any heavier, it was now an undeniable torrent, falling in sheets with low visibility, giant drops bouncing violently off the ground. He could not even bring his horse to a full gallop for fear that he might inadvertently collide with the young woman for whom he searched.

Even with his heavy coat, Darcy felt the urge to shiver as the cold and merciless rain fell upon him. He was not certain how much of the chill could be attributed to his anxiety over how Miss Elizabeth must have been feeling. Was she frightened? Had she found shelter of some kind?

Finally, blessing of blessings, he heard a cry of pain over the din of rain. For a moment, he thought he had imagined it, but then he grew more certain that he had heard correctly, and he dismounted, leaving his horse behind to search for the source of the sound.

And then he found it—found *her*. She was but a blur of yellow and white upon the ground, but he knew immediately it was Elizabeth Bennet. She had collapsed upon the grass and weeds, and her dress was utterly drenched, but as she swiped at her face with wet gloves, he knew she would be fine.

"Miss Bennet," said he, his voice sounding hoarse as he spoke. He only realized how fast his heart had been racing now that it began to slow down. "Miss Bennet, are you well?"

Her bonnet did little to keep the rain out of her eyes, so she was forced to use a hand to shield her face from the rain plummeting down upon her in order to look at him. "Mr. Darcy?"

"Yes," said he with a relieved smile. Then he asked her again, "Miss Bennet, are you well?"

Trembling with the cold, she gave a weak chuckle. "My ankle and my dignity are both hurt, but I suppose I shall not perish from either."

He knelt beside her. "Which ankle, Miss Bennet?"

She made a vague sort of gesture, and he reached down to brush aside her skirt and feel her ankle through her stocking. He tested its movement, and though she obviously felt pained by the motion, she suppressed any cries.

"It is swollen," said he, "but I do not believe it is broken."

Their eyes met and held then, their proximity enabling them to see each other despite the downpour. Darcy felt his breath catch in his throat, and he realized, rather belatedly, that he should not have been touching her ankle in such an intimate way. He withdrew his hands abruptly, as if burned.

After clearing his throat, he said quietly: "I beg your pardon, Miss Bennet."

She flushed and turned her head, nodding but not giving a verbal response.

Darcy thought her trembling was increasing, and he took off his coat and draped it around her shoulders. "It may not do much to protect you from the rain," said he, "but perhaps it will provide some aid."

The young woman nodded and murmured her thanks.

"I will have to beg your pardon once again, Miss Bennet, for I must lift you," said Mr. Darcy. Then, before waiting for a response, he scooped her up and got to his feet.

Miss Elizabeth let out a gasp of surprise at the sudden movement, but she did not protest. Instead, she hesitated for a moment before she raised her arms and put them around his neck. His jacket slid off her shoulders as she did so, though it remained pinned between them and did not fall to the ground.

In other circumstances, Darcy might have relished in the feeling of holding Miss Elizabeth in his arms, and indeed, he could not fully repine the events that had led them to that point. Though both he and the young woman were soaked to the bone, he could feel a tingle of warmth where her wet gloves touched his neck. There had been a few terrifying minutes where he had been certain that something terrible had happened to her. Now that he knew she was safe, he could feel nothing but relief and joy.

He carried Miss Elizabeth to his horse, and after warning her, he lifted her onto the creature. He then returned his coat to her and watched as she put her arms through the sleeves. She gave him a wry smile, and he nodded at her in approval. She may have thought herself to be a ridiculous sight, but he felt a sense of warmth and protectiveness arise within him as he gazed upon her.

After ensuring that Miss Elizabeth seemed to be secure, Darcy mounted behind her, bringing his arms around her to take the reins in hand. Once more, he felt filled with a sense of rightness.

Darcy turned the horse toward Haskett Hall, and as they moved forward, Miss Elizabeth shivered in his arms.

"You need not worry, Miss Bennet," said he into her ear. "It shall not be long before we have returned to the house."

She murmured something unintelligible in response, but he saw no need to make her repeat herself due to the roar of the rain.

When the house came into view at last, Darcy felt a sense of disappointment mingled with relief. But he did not dwell on those emotions. Rather, he dismounted and insisted upon carrying Miss Elizabeth into the house despite her weak protests. Based on her trembling, he suspected she might not have been able to carry herself forward even if she had tried.

When Mr. Darcy walked through the front doors of Haskett Hall with Elizabeth in his arms, Mrs. Williamson let out a cry of relief.

"Mr. Darcy! Miss Elizabeth! Oh, dear, you are both drenched beyond belief!"

Clucking, the housekeeper then assisted in divesting them of a few pieces of their outdoor apparel, removing Elizabeth's bonnet and taking Mr. Darcy's hat. She seemed to hesitate over whether to take Mr. Darcy's coat from Elizabeth before finally deciding to leave it.

Mrs. Williamson's cries had alerted others in the house, and Jane and Kitty rushed out of the drawing-room with Lady Catherine behind them.

"Lizzy!" cried both sisters in relief.

"Are you well?" asked Jane.

"You should not have done that," said Kitty.

"What a foolish girl," added Lady Catherine.

Elizabeth let out a halfhearted laugh, embarrassed by all the attention and by the fact that Mr. Darcy still had not set her down. "My ankle and my vanity have been temporarily wounded by my foolishness, certainly, but I am otherwise well. At least, I shall be once I have been given the opportunity to warm myself by the fire."

"A young lady such as yourself should never go walking outside alone," said Lady Catherine in a disapproving tone, "particularly when the weather bodes ill."

"Now, now," said Mrs. Williamson, "I think the young lady does not need to be scolded any further. I believe what she needs most is to be dried off and allowed to rest. Mr. Darcy, might you be so kind as to carry her to her room? I am not certain where Billy and Mr. Wickham are, or I would ask one of them to aid you."

"There is no need," said Mr. Darcy. "I shall gladly perform the office myself."

Then Mr. Darcy carried Elizabeth to her chambers, where he set her down upon a chair at Mrs. Williamson's prompting. Then the older woman shooed him out of the room, allowing only Elizabeth's two sisters and Lady Catherine to remain with her.

With fumbling but well-meaning effort, Mrs. Williamson, Jane, and Kitty aided Elizabeth in changing into different clothes and drying off her hair. Lady Catherine attempted to dictate their efforts, but her commands were ignored in favor of what was most expedient.

When Elizabeth was finally dry and felt more like herself, she shyly gestured toward Mr. Darcy's coat, which had been placed nearby, and requested that Mrs. Williamson see that it was returned to Mr. Darcy.

"Of course, my dear," said Mrs. Williamson warmly, pressing Elizabeth's arm. She then ushered Elizabeth into her bed and drew up the bed-covering, clucking all the while.

Though Elizabeth's ankle still hurt, and she felt a chill deep inside her bones, she was otherwise no worse for the wear, and she felt thankful that she had been found so quickly by Mr. Darcy.

When her sisters supported the commands of Lady Catherine and Mrs. Williamson for Elizabeth to stay in bed, Elizabeth only made a few token complaints about their heavy-handedness. In truth, she felt weary enough that the notion of remaining in bed could only be welcomed. And when Jane said tenderly, "I shall even fetch you a book, Lizzy," Elizabeth felt her heart become warm, and she decided to relent to whatever was requested of her. She had missed her loving relationship with Jane, and even this small glimpse of what they had once shared was enough to bring her joy.

Chapter XIII

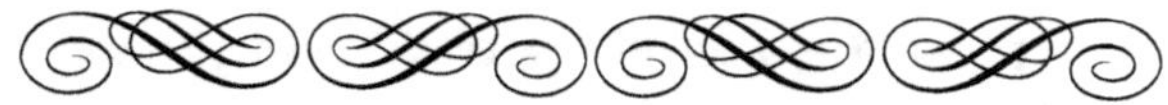

One day's rest was quite enough for Elizabeth, and though her ankle still seemed disinclined to allow her to bear weight on it without assaulting her with agony, she insisted upon sitting in the drawing-room with the rest of the Haskett Hall company.

The drawing-room felt rather crowded that day. Seated with the women were Mr. Darcy, Mr. Wickham, and Mr. Bingley, and all appeared to be anxious about Elizabeth's well-being in some form. The sight of Mr. Wickham in particular was a surprise, as a steward would not typically have been mingling with higher company in such a fashion, but Elizabeth supposed his presence could only be attributed to Henry Darcy's preference for the man's company. As for Henry Darcy himself, he was present as well, and he smirked any time Mr. Darcy or Mr. Wickham spoke to Elizabeth. She was mystified as to why, but she did not like to humor him when she could avoid it, so she decided not to inquire as to the reason for his amusement.

While Elizabeth attempted to involve herself with a volume of poetry, Mr. Wickham chose to speak to her once more. "What precisely has caught your interest, Miss Elizabeth?"

"I believe you have some work to do, Wickham," said Mr. Darcy curtly. "Might it be a better use of your time if you were to tend to it?"

"Oh, I finished what you requested of me already, Darcy. You need not worry."

"Actually, I would like to discuss that very work with you, Wickham. Please come with me."

Mr. Wickham's lip twitched, and he glanced between Mr. Darcy and Elizabeth as if attempting to decide whether to comply, but he finally sighed and stood. Giving a bow, he looked at Elizabeth and said:

"I suppose I may as well do as he says, or I shall never hear the end of it."

Then Mr. Darcy escorted Mr. Wickham hastily from the room.

Once they had retreated, Henry Darcy began to guffaw.

Elizabeth raised her brow, finally unable to restrain herself from speaking to the man. "Might I inquire as to what precisely you find to be so amusing?"

"Lizzy," said Jane quietly in warning.

Elizabeth, however, feigned not to hear and stared expectantly at Mr. Henry Darcy.

His mirth did not abate, and he responded with an unoffended grin. "I never thought I would witness the day when Fitz would be afflicted with such envy—and over a woman, nonetheless."

"I am afraid I do not catch your meaning, sir," said Elizabeth.

"Then perhaps I should spell it out clearly for you. My brother detests it when Wickham flirts with you. That is why Fitz could not remove Wickham from this room fast enough."

Elizabeth found that her mouth refused to issue forth any words. Based on Mr. Darcy's volatile relationship with Mr. Wickham, she would not have expected him to support Mr. Wickham's flirtations with any proper young woman. However, for Mr. Darcy's dislike to be the product of envy seemed a veritably ludicrous notion.

Kitty soon spoke in Elizabeth's place. "Perhaps Mr. Darcy is merely trying to ensure your friend remains focused on estate management. Mr. Wickham *is* your steward, after all."

Henry Darcy shrugged. "My brother can have more than one reason for what he does."

"If they are discussing your estate, then perhaps it would be wise of you to join them," said Mr. Bingley suddenly.

"Mr. Bingley's suggestion is a sound one," said Lady Catherine, "and I would recommend that you abide by it."

She glanced from the Bennet sisters to her nephew, a slight frown on her face. "I should have thought you would act in a more proper manner than this, Henry."

The young man sighed. "I had expected Bingley to take Fitz's side, but I suppose I should also have expected the same from your ladyship. Very well. I know when I am not welcome among company. I shall find some other way to occupy myself."

Mr. Henry Darcy stood to leave, and no one attempted to stop him. Before he left the room, however, he paused and looked at the company. "I suppose I should ask for leave from my *beloved* fiancée." He then glanced at Mr. Bingley. "But I do not think I shall be missed."

Before Jane or anyone else could respond, he had disappeared from the room.

Elizabeth turned her gaze to Mr. Bingley. The man appeared as close to angry as she had ever seen him, his mouth tight and his fists clenched as he attempted to calm himself. As for Jane, she remained quiet and seemingly unaffected, her attention having turned to her embroidery.

Kitty appeared to be less inclined to refrain from commenting on the man's rudeness. "Someone needs to teach Mr. Henry Darcy to mind his tongue."

While it might ordinarily have been expedient to curb such comments in a setting that included the aunt of their target, Elizabeth found her irritation had reached such a level that she had no desire to do so.

Mr. Bingley also appeared to be under no compunction concerning speaking ill of Henry Darcy in Lady Catherine's presence. "Indeed, someone does. There are those who deserve much better treatment than that which he offers."

Surprisingly, her ladyship did not voice any disagreement. In truth, she might not have even heard what was said, as she stared steadfastly at the door Mr. Henry Darcy had used to exit the room, a frown affixed to her face.

Recalling Caroline Livingston's words, Elizabeth could only agree that Mr. Bingley did love Jane. It would have been much better if Jane had been required to marry *him* rather than Mr. Henry Darcy, but there was no sense in making wishes that would never take flight.

Elizabeth soon found her mind wandering to the eldest Darcy. Apart from some similarity in the structure of their face and the color of their hair, Mr. Darcy could scarcely be more dissimilar from his brother. Due to their societal stature, both men must have been spoiled as children, but she supposed that while the elder of the two had taken on the mantle of responsibility, the younger had shirked it entirely, doing as he pleased. Henry Darcy made for a terrible match with Jane, who would never venture to escape even the smallest of her responsibilities.

Perhaps the elder Mr. Darcy would have been a better match with Jane. That thought, however, was fleeting, as Elizabeth immediately began to reconsider it. His somber attitude would not have paired well with Jane's quiet elegance. Mr. Darcy would surely benefit from marrying someone who possessed a livelier disposition.

That thought lightened her heart slightly, though she could not be certain why.

The next day marked the arrival of Georgiana Darcy and her companion, Mrs. Annesley. Miss Darcy's great reticence became quickly apparent to Elizabeth, but so did the young woman's love for her brothers. Miss Darcy appeared to have a particularly special relationship with Henry, who immediately took the opportunity to lift her in the air and spin her around as if she were as heavy as a leaf.

"You have grown so much taller, Georgie," cried he. His face bore the first heartfelt smile Elizabeth had seen upon it. "I can scarcely believe I am related to such a giant as this."

"*Henry,*" said Miss Darcy in a slight admonishment, her voice quiet but her returning smile broad.

"I wondered whether Fitz might be teasing me when he said you would come, but I see now that he spoke only truth. I am glad for it."

Miss Darcy's head dipped, her shyness in company coming forth once more, but her happiness was more than plain.

Elizabeth had never expected to find Henry to be such a doting brother, and the realization caused a slight alteration in her perception of him. If he could behave in such a congenial manner with his sister, then perhaps he could even grow to love his wife. Elizabeth felt hope rising in her heart.

After introductions had been properly made, Lady Catherine took a moment to speak directly to Miss Darcy. "Dear girl, I am quite proud of your bearing. Mrs. Annesley must have been encouraging you, for you are not as apt to stoop and hide as you once were. Have you continued your practice upon the pianoforte?"

Miss Darcy murmured a confirmation, and upon realizing that Miss Darcy's shy nature extended even to her interactions with some of her relations, Elizabeth resolved to do what she could to coax her out of her shyness.

The next day, the party was gathered in the drawing-room when Elizabeth noticed Miss Darcy eyeing the pianoforte with an unmistakable fondness.

Recalling Lady Catherine's question to Miss Darcy about the instrument, Elizabeth addressed the young woman with: "Do you enjoying playing the pianoforte, Miss Darcy?"

The girl seemed startled at having been addressed, but she recovered quickly. "I do indeed, but I lack the courage to play in front of anyone but my family."

"That must be quite the shame," said Elizabeth, "for I imagine you must have a prodigious talent. I, however, have no talent at all, but I shall gladly play for anyone who asks—after I have demonstrated the proper demurral, of course."

Miss Darcy's unease seemed to recede a fraction. "I imagine you are skilled at the pianoforte in spite of your words, Miss Elizabeth. However, I must own to some curiosity, if you shall forgive my boldness. Why would a person who professes no skill be eager to comply with a request to play?"

The way Miss Darcy's eyes darted away after asking the question made Elizabeth think the girl had regretted doing so, but Elizabeth gave a warm reply. "Why, if I can make someone laugh, then I consider my meager talents to be a success, even if that laughter might be focused upon me. Perhaps it is a demonstration of vanity of a sort, but I always strive to be lively in company."

"Could you—that is, would you mind playing?" asked Miss Darcy with a shy smile.

"I would not mind playing if you would consent to serve as my page-turner."

Miss Darcy glanced around at the others in the room with obvious nervousness, but she finally nodded and indicated her agreement.

Elizabeth ushered her over to the pianoforte while talking about a few inconsequential items to ease Miss Darcy's discomfort. Though Elizabeth's ankle remained tender, she now found it no chore to walk upon it for short distances, and she was glad that her movement to the pianoforte would produce no visible signs that would cause Miss Darcy to feel concerned.

After finally settling in and selecting a piece, Elizabeth turned to the young woman.

"Are you ready to begin, Miss Darcy?"

"I am indeed," said Miss Darcy quietly.

Smiling broadly, Elizabeth set to playing the instrument. She had not been diligent in her practice in recent times, so she made even more mistakes than was her usual wont. Still, she retained her smile and said to Miss Darcy:

"You must no doubt have noticed my fingers scampering over certain wrong notes. You may feel free to chuckle at the evidence of my lack of practice without fear of offending me."

"I would do no such thing, Miss Elizabeth," said the girl. "I rather find your lively music to be pleasant to hear."

"You are too kind, Miss Darcy. I should much prefer for my audience to always be composed of young women as generous as you have shown yourself to be. With the exception of Jane, all of my sisters scruple not to tell me whenever I tread upon a disharmonious note."

"You know *I* would do no such thing, Lizzy," said Kitty from across the room. "I can barely string two lines of music together, and I would not know it even if you did choose notes in error."

Elizabeth smiled and bowed her head slightly. "It is true that not all of my sisters are fluent with the language of music."

"Did you not have tutors?" asked Miss Darcy, her curiosity lending her a moment of bravery.

"Those who wished to learn could," said Elizabeth, "but we were never provided the sort of structure that you have likely experienced in your life."

"A young woman's life can benefit greatly from structure," said Mr. Darcy from nearby.

Elizabeth glanced at him, not having realized he had approached them. Though she had to turn her eyes back to the instrument in front of her, she replied to the gentleman.

"Certainly, it can, Mr. Darcy, but there is also something to be said for letting young women choose some of their own pursuits. After all, a man who finds himself attracted to a woman based solely on her ability to cover a screen will find himself disappointed if her wit cannot approach at least the swiftness of a mouse, if not a hare."

"Nonetheless, there is something to be said for feminine accomplishments," returned Mr. Darcy, "is there not?"

"A woman should be able to make herself of use to contribute to the working of her household, but being in possession of several handfuls of accomplishments is no better than having a few which she truly enjoys."

"I do enjoy playing the pianoforte when I am alone," said Miss Darcy quietly, as if uncertain how to best take part in the conversation.

"Then I believe it is the best of your accomplishments," said Elizabeth, "even if no one else ever hears you."

Miss Darcy gave a shy smile before she returned her attention to turning pages for Elizabeth.

Once the piece of music was over, Miss Darcy and Mr. Darcy both praised Elizabeth's playing.

"I have not often taken this much pleasure in listening to the music of another," said Miss Darcy.

"Indeed, the experience is one I should not hesitate to repeat," said Mr. Darcy.

"Ah!" said Elizabeth. "You have both chosen foolishly to stroke my vanity. Do you not know that a dog who has been fed a bounty of scraps shall never leave and shall only beg for more?"

Miss Darcy appeared horrified by her words and protested: "I should never think to make such a comparison, Miss Elizabeth. My praise was genuine and heartfelt."

"You need not be alarmed, Georgiana," said Mr. Darcy, "for Miss Elizabeth enjoys making light of her own talents."

Elizabeth smiled. "Certainly, I would not deny that."

"Miss Elizabeth, you must know that there are few people who would ever wish for you to depart from them," said Mr. Darcy, "so if scraps must be provided to encourage your continued presence, then I shall gladly provide them."

As Elizabeth closed the music in front of her, she noticed in the periphery that Miss Darcy appeared to be peering at her brother. When Elizabeth glanced at him to see his expression, she saw him smiling at her. Elizabeth soon found herself smiling back at him.

She and Miss Darcy both stood, and Mr. Darcy joined the rest of the party.

Quietly, Elizabeth said: "Miss Darcy, I hope you may soon consider me to be your friend."

Miss Darcy, in a fit of boldness, pressed her hand and murmured: "Oh, Miss Bennet, I will gladly befriend any woman who can make Fitzwilliam appear to be so happy."

As Miss Darcy walked away to sit with the company, Elizabeth frowned, not certain precisely what to make of the young woman's words.

CHAPTER XIV

The next week passed in a pleasant enough fashion. There was tension between the male Darcys and Mr. Wickham, but Mr. Henry Darcy remained on his best behavior, and Elizabeth began to believe that there could be hope yet for the marriage between him and Jane—if only Georgiana Darcy could remain at Haskett Hall with them.

Elizabeth and Kitty both especially enjoyed the young woman's company. Georgiana was slightly younger than Kitty, but she demonstrated such a maturity that Kitty appeared to take notice and modify her own behavior accordingly. Soon, Georgiana found herself laughing in their presence and smiling brightly whenever she walked into a room and saw them. The young women even agreed to call each other by their Christian names, which only made Georgiana seem all the happier.

One evening, Elizabeth remained in the drawing-room much later than was her habit, as she was caught within the pages of a book, and soon, all had left the room save Mrs. Annesley. Once Elizabeth realized how distracted she had been, she felt her cheeks turn warm.

"I suppose I should have joined the others in readying myself for bed," said Elizabeth, shaking her head in self-deprecation.

"Oh, you need not worry, Miss Elizabeth," said Mrs. Annesley. "I had hoped to have a moment alone with you anyway, so I am glad that you have remained this long."

"Is that so?"

"It is indeed. I wished to thank you for your efforts in befriending Georgiana. She is a dear girl, but I have been worried about her for some time. When the elder Mr. Darcy and his wife died, it took a toll on all their children, but I believe Georgiana found the situation especially trying. After all, she was left with two brothers and little female companionship from girls of an age with her.

"As you have seen, both of Georgiana's brothers are protective, but while she has not lacked affection from them, they have not allowed her to move freely in company. As such, her discomfort with new acquaintances can be quite extreme."

"I had noticed her reticence," said Elizabeth with a smile.

Mrs. Annesley chuckled. "Yes, as anyone would. Of course, Mr. Darcy is uncomfortable in company as well, yet he certainly seems to enjoy himself when you are around. Perhaps you are merely skilled in soothing the unease of the Darcys."

Elizabeth raised a brow. "If that were so, then I would have exercised that power on Mr. Henry Darcy some time ago."

"I do not believe anyone in England can control that young man," said the older woman as she shook her head, "except, of course, his sister, but only to a certain extent."

"I had noticed the effect she had on him."

"She may very well be the only reason he has not run the Darcy name into the ground. But I suppose I should not have even said that much."

"I shall hold everything in confidence, so you need not worry."

"I know," said Mrs. Annesley. She gestured to the sewing in which she had been engrossed. "I suppose it is time for me to set this aside and put these tired bones to bed."

"I shall not be too much longer," said Elizabeth, holding up the book she had in hand. "I have a few more pages to read, and then I shall be finished."

Mrs. Annesley pressed Elizabeth's hand and then took her leave.

For a few minutes, Elizabeth returned her concentration to the volume that had been holding her interest. She finally read the last page and released the contented sigh of one who had just completed a book.

Holding the precious volume to herself, Elizabeth moved forward and started to proceed through the doorway—

—only for the sudden appearance of a male form to cause her to lurch backward in fright.

"Mr. Wickham!" cried she after realizing who stood before her. "I thought you had retired for the night."

"Well," said he, staggering as he tried to look at her, "you can see I did not."

As he leered over her, Elizabeth took a few steps backward into the drawing-room. A brief whiff revealed that the man reeked of alcohol. The ruddiness of his cheeks only further served to confirm his physical state of intoxication.

"I beg your pardon, Mr. Wickham," said Elizabeth, trying to determine how to move around the man without shoving him aside, "but I was about to retire to my room."

"Oh, I don' think that's necess'ry," said he as he entered the room and fumbled to close the door behind him.

"It is, Mr. Wickham, and you are blocking the path," said Elizabeth, her alarm growing.

"I thought you might want a chance to enjoy yours'lf," said he with a sickening grin as he advanced.

Elizabeth glanced at the now-closed door and took a breath to steady herself. "It is not appropriate for us to be alone in a room together, sir."

Mr. Wickham reached out to grab her. She darted around him and flung herself at the door. She turned the knob with a shaky hand and then practically leaped out the door.

Mr. Wickham was right behind her and grabbed her arm. He tugged at it, but she resisted him.

"Mr. Wickham, release me!" cried she, struggling to free herself.

"Come, 'Lizabeth," said Mr. Wickham, trying to pull her toward the drawing-room. "Have you no desire for a bit o' fun?"

"Unhand her!" cried a male voice from down the hall, causing Elizabeth and Mr. Wickham to turn their heads toward the sound.

Elizabeth nearly melted in relief as she realized it was Mr. Darcy who had called out. Unfortunately, the appearance of the other man did not serve as a sufficient incentive for Mr. Wickham to relax his grip, and he only tightened the hold of his fingers on Elizabeth's arm.

Mr. Darcy drew up beside them in moments, and he grabbed Mr. Wickham by his lapels with a fierce scowl. "Release her *now*."

Mr. Wickham's fingers slowly relinquished Elizabeth's arm, and she pulled it back to herself and held it, scarcely able to believe her narrow escape.

Still clutching the other man's coat, Mr. Darcy spoke in low but menacing tones as he glared at Mr. Wickham with enough heat to cause even a king to cower beneath his gaze. "I allowed my brother to keep you as his steward out of respect for your late father and mine, but you have now proven yourself to be beyond hope entirely. You will vacate the property immediately."

Mr. Wickham seemed to have sobered somewhat, but his voice shook a little as he responded. "You will regret tossing me out, Darcy."

Ignoring the threat, Mr. Darcy said: "Though it is more consideration than you deserve, I will see to it that your belongings are sent to the local inn."

Mr. Wickham stared at the other man, as if he intended to argue, but he must have thought better of it, as he replied with: "Very well. But I must insist on taking a few of my possessions now before I am tossed out of the house."

As Mr. Wickham stalked away, Elizabeth turned to Mr. Darcy. Her legs felt unsteady, but she was not of such a weak disposition as to faint from the shock of what had happened. "I cannot express how grateful I am for your fortuitous arrival."

"And I cannot express how sorry I am that you were thrust into such deplorable circumstances in my brother's house." The anger Mr. Darcy felt toward Mr. Wickham was evinced by the tightness of his jaw and the heaviness of his breathing, and Elizabeth found herself touched that he would feel so strongly on her account.

"Well, you prevented the circumstances from worsening," said Elizabeth lightly, "and for that, I thank you."

Mr. Darcy gave her a slight nod in acknowledgment of her gratitude, but his eyes shifted to look in the direction in which Mr. Wickham had disappeared. "I need to advise my brother about what happened with his steward. Would you mind finding a manservant to oversee Mr. Wickham's departure?"

Elizabeth agreed to do so, and she and Mr. Darcy parted. She called for the housekeeper and explained the situation, and the distraught Mrs. Williamson promised to send Mr. Montgomery to watch over Mr. Wickham.

Feeling more at ease now, Elizabeth once more began to take a path back to her bed chambers. This time, however, she could not help but rub her arm repeatedly, as if there were a stain present that could not be scrubbed out.

Darcy could not recall ever having been as angry as he felt that evening. If he had decided to retire to bed early instead of endeavoring to attend to some estate business, then a wretched fate could have befallen Elizabeth Bennet, and he would never have been able to forgive himself.

Darcy had intended for Haskett Hall to serve as a haven of sorts for the Bennet sisters—a way for them to see Henry in a slightly different light and for them to be comforted by the realization that Henry could comport himself better when away from the tainted claws of the London elite. The endeavor had been a disaster, however, starting with Henry's mistress and then culminating with Wickham's lechery. Darcy now wished they had never left London.

Darcy found Henry in the study, holding up a glass and gazing ponderously at the remaining amber liquid contained within.

"Fitz," greeted Henry, refusing to look away from his drink.

"I will withstand Wickham's presence no longer," said Darcy bluntly. "I have instructed him to leave the premises."

Those words caused Henry to look at Darcy. He tilted his head in confusion as he studied his brother's face. "What has you up in arms?"

"I caught that drunkard harassing Miss Elizabeth. If he puts a hand on her again, I shall remove it from his body forthright."

Henry grimaced. "I warned him to leave her alone because of your interest in her. But he was in here drinking with me not that long ago, so you should afford him a little leeway with regard to his behavior."

"I refuse to do anything of the sort. I withstood that man's presence solely due to my father's respect for the elder Mr. Wickham, but I refuse to do so any longer. Even if you disregard that man's utter lack of morals, you cannot dispute the fact that you need a capable steward. Wickham has only been feeding into your bad habits. I told him to leave, and I meant it. Once he gathers a bag's worth of belongings, he will be gone from this house. I will have the rest of his things sent to him later."

Henry raised an eyebrow. "Need I remind you that it is not exactly your place to dismiss my steward?"

"The only reason Haskett Hall is not in complete shambles is because of the work performed by me and *my own* steward. If you want me to withdraw all my support and let your current lifestyle collapse in upon itself, then so be it."

Henry set his drink aside and stared at Darcy for a long moment. "I suppose you are serious about this, then."

"I am."

"Well," said Henry, "I have had a bit to drink, so I think it might be better if we discuss this in the morning."

"I will not change my mind," said Darcy in warning. Then he swept out of the room.

He would not be forgetting any time soon the frightened look on Miss Elizabeth's face as she had been held by that reprehensible snake.

CHAPTER XV

Though Elizabeth retired to her room shortly after speaking to the housekeeper, she found herself tossing and turning in her bed next to Kitty, unable to sleep.

Her mind kept returning to Mr. Wickham's assault on her person. His grip on her arm had been tight and unyielding, and she would not be surprised to see a bruise result from it. Mr. Darcy's timely appearance had been such a blessing.

She was just as thankful that the experience had involved her rather than Jane or Kitty. Jane might not have been able to fend off the man's advances, and Kitty was young enough that she might have been fooled by Wickham, even if his drunken state had been obvious. It probably would not have taken much for him to fill her head with nonsense.

Though Elizabeth found her mind to be preoccupied, the room remained quiet enough that the sound of a distressed female voice outside her door caused her to sit up. After glancing at Kitty and weighing her options, Elizabeth decided to investigate the sound.

She lowered her feet to the floor and quickly wrapped a shawl around her. Then she opened the door and peered out. Upon seeing only Georgiana Darcy, she stepped out into the hallway.

"Georgiana?" asked she quietly.

The girl turned toward her, her face the image of distress as she clutched a letter to herself. The distress transitioned into relief at the sight of Elizabeth. "Oh, Elizabeth!"

"Are you well?" asked Elizabeth, attempting to prompt an explanation of the reason for Georgiana's upset.

"Oh, it is simply this letter," said Georgiana, her chin quivering as she glanced down at the piece of correspondence she held.

Slowly, Elizabeth asked: "Might I inquire as to who wrote the letter?"

"I received it from Mr. Montgomery. He is Mr. Wickham's friend and one of the servants here, so Mr. Wickham asked him to give it to me on his behalf. It is—it is from Mr. Wickham."

A sense of alarm rose within Elizabeth. "You know that is not proper, Georgiana. What does it say?"

"I know it is not proper," said Georgiana as she nodded repeatedly. "I know. But what it says is—"

"What does it say?" asked Elizabeth gently.

Whispering in a halting voice, Georgiana replied: "It describes Mr. Wickham's long-held admiration of me. Elizabeth, I have long been . . . charmed by his manners, but I had not the slightest idea that . . . that he may have ever noticed me."

"You need not be surprised that someone is charmed by you, but I suspect your distress has a different cause."

"It does," said Georgiana, now in tears. "He wishes for me to meet him and elope with him to Gretna Green." Her hand shaking, she held the letter out for Elizabeth to take.

As she accepted the proffered letter, Elizabeth realized she and Mr. Darcy should have anticipated that Mr. Wickham would be the good friend of any servant sent to watch over him. Still, her heart broke for the innocent Georgiana, who had no idea that Mr. Wickham was using her as nothing more than a form of revenge. "Oh, Georgiana—"

"But I know my brothers would be disappointed if I were to leave with Mr. Wickham," said Georgiana. "I should never wish to cause them any pain."

"I am glad to hear that, and I am certain they would be as well. But dear Georgiana, an honorable man would never ask you to disappear with him in the dead of night without advising anyone of your departure. He wishes to take you with him merely because he has been relieved of his position as steward by your eldest brother. Mr. Wickham is attempting to cause Mr. Darcy pain by taking you away from here. Both of your brothers would be heartbroken if you were to fall into the hands of such a dishonorable man."

Georgiana's tears only worsened at that point, and she buried her face in her hands, unable to speak. Though still holding the offensive piece of correspondence, Elizabeth put her arms around Georgiana and gently patted her back. "You have not left with him, Georgiana, so no damage has been done. You need not continue weeping. As long as you have no intent to leave, there is no cause for concern."

Georgiana made a noise that appeared to be agreement.

"Now, come sit in my room to calm yourself while I put on some more appropriate clothes, and then we shall go speak to Mr. Darcy."

Georgiana shook her head, clasping her hands together. Then, speaking in gasps that were punctuated with sobs, she begged:

"Please, Elizabeth, may we speak to Henry instead? If Fitzwilliam is already angry with Mr. Wickham, then I fear his reaction. His temper can grow quite hot."

Though Elizabeth was less than fond of Henry Darcy, she knew he had a good relationship with his sister, so she readily assented to help soothe the girl. Then she returned to her room with Georgiana accompanying her.

Kitty sat up in bed, blinking, when they made their entrance, but Elizabeth merely told her to return to sleep. After Elizabeth set the letter aside and put on clothes more appropriate for a conversation with her future brother-in-law, she took the correspondence in hand once more and left the room with a slightly calmer Georgiana.

They soon stood in front of the door to the room belonging to the master of the house, and Elizabeth did not hesitate to make an urgent rap upon it.

Henry appeared to be rather bleary and out of sorts when he answered the door in his nightclothes. At the sight of Elizabeth, his eyes narrowed in irritation, but then he saw Georgiana standing behind her, and the irritation faded away. He entered the hall as Elizabeth stepped backward, and he looked at his sister.

"Has something happened, Georgie?"

Georgiana rushed forward to embrace her brother, sobbing into his shirt.

Elizabeth saw how his arms immediately came up to encircle his sister, further tempering her ill feelings toward him. After observing him for a moment, she said: "Your former steward asked Mr. Montgomery to deliver a rather inappropriate letter to Georgiana."

It took a moment for her words to come together in Henry Darcy's head, but he finally managed a response. "Wickham wrote to Georgie?"

"In his letter, Mr. Wickham professed holding tender feelings toward Georgiana and requested that she elope with him to Gretna Green," said Elizabeth. "I am certain that you understand his actions are a result of his anger with your brother rather than any emotional attachment to your sister."

Henry Darcy released a hissing sound. From the contortions of his mouth, Elizabeth could only guess that he was making a prodigious effort to refrain from cursing in front of his sister. He finally could not continue holding himself back.

"That wanton windsucker!" cried he. "I will make him rue the day he ever stepped foot in Haskett Hall."

As Mr. Henry Darcy attempted to extricate himself from his sister's grasp, Georgiana began to sob harder.

"No, Henry! Please do not go!"

But the girl could not compete with his strength, and he broke free of her hold on him and disappeared into his room. Elizabeth supposed he meant to dress before seeking out Mr. Wickham, yet she had an ill feeling about it.

The crescendo of Georgiana's sobs soon became a full-blown wail, and she collapsed on the floor. Elizabeth knelt beside her, trying to calm her and wishing she had chosen to speak to Mr. Darcy despite Georgiana's pleas.

Soon, the object of her thoughts appeared, no doubt drawn by the noise being made by Georgiana.

"Miss Bennet, what has happened to my sister?" asked Mr. Darcy, his voice low and concerned.

Elizabeth glanced at Georgiana for some sort of directive, but the girl refused to look up from where she was crying into her hands. At last, Elizabeth stood and explained everything, from what had happened with Mr. Wickham to what Mr. Henry Darcy had resolved to do.

Mr. Darcy's expression darkened as she made her explanation. When she had finished, he asked no further questions. Instead, he merely said: "Please try to stop my brother from leaving. I shall return."

Elizabeth released a soft sigh as he left. Mr. Darcy had been in his nightclothes, so he no doubt meant to change and accompany his brother to confront Mr. Wickham. She could only hope that the more level-headed nature of Mr. Darcy would serve to counteract the destructive anger of his younger brother.

Elizabeth sat on the floor beside Georgiana and put an arm around her, making hushing sounds. With her other hand, she held Mr. Wickham's letter, which she quickly read, knowing that the Darcy men would request information concerning where Mr. Wickham had intended to meet Georgiana.

When Mr. Henry Darcy appeared, having hastily dressed, he demanded to know where Mr. Wickham awaited Georgiana's appearance. After telling him, Elizabeth said: "Your brother has asked that you wait for him. I believe he wants to go with you."

"I refuse to allow Wickham another moment to escape the reckoning he so rightly deserves," said the man. Heedless of Elizabeth's protests and Georgiana's tearful pleas, he stormed off.

Between sobs, Georgiana inquired of Elizabeth: "What will happen to Henry?"

Elizabeth feared that very thing, but she knew that frightening Georgiana further could do no good, so she attempted instead to calm her.

"He loves you very much, Georgiana. He will do what he feels he must to protect you."

"We should n-never have told my brothers."

"No, dear Georgiana, that is not true," said Elizabeth, desperate to keep the girl's anguish from increasing. "They needed to know. They need to ensure that Mr. Wickham will not try to pursue you further."

"But if something happens to them—"

"Shh, shh," said Elizabeth. "Please, do not worry. They would not wish for you to concern yourself with that."

Georgiana embraced Elizabeth tightly, no doubt desperate for consolation.

When Mr. Darcy appeared, a feeling of foreboding had begun to grow within Elizabeth. She attempted to push it aside, yet she feared the worst.

"Your brother refused to wait," said she, looking up at Mr. Darcy.

He shook his head, obviously aggravated. "Could you please tell me where he went, Miss Bennet?"

Once Elizabeth passed on the directions from Mr. Wickham's letter, Mr. Darcy gave a curt nod. "Thank you for your assistance. I fear I have not been thinking clearly. Could you please wake up Bingley and ask him to watch over Georgiana as well as you and your sisters? I do not think Wickham will return to the house, but I believe it would be better to take precautions."

"I will do so," said Elizabeth.

Mr. Darcy leaned down to squeeze his sister's shoulder, and he said softly: "Do not worry, Georgiana."

Then he left them.

Elizabeth helped a trembling Georgiana to her feet, and they went to rouse Mr. Bingley. He listened to them as he stood in his nightclothes, and then he suggested they retrieve Elizabeth's sisters while he changed into more appropriate attire.

Elizabeth found that her sisters had already been awoken by the commotion, and she assisted in helping them hastily dress. Mr. Bingley awaited them in the hallway when they finished, and he ushered them into the drawing-room, advising that he wished for them to remain comfortable while they waited.

"I suppose we may as well awaken Lady Catherine and Mrs. Annesley," said Elizabeth after glancing around at the bleary-eyed party. Lady Catherine would no doubt be upset upon realizing what had been unfolding without her, and Mrs. Annesley might be able to assist in comforting Georgiana. "Mr. Bingley, would you mind watching over Georgiana and my sisters?"

"I should be glad to do so," said he, "but please return quickly."

"I will," said Elizabeth.

Georgiana's mortification appeared to increase at the notion of having further witnesses to what had happened, but Elizabeth knew nothing could be done to keep the knowledge from the two older women. She only hoped that the two Darcy men were having an easier time than their sister was.

CHAPTER XVI

Henry spurred on his horse faster than he ever had before, driving it to the outskirts of the Haskett Hall grounds with a single-minded ferocity. As he approached, he saw Wickham standing beside his own horse, skulking in the darkness and awaiting the arrival of dear little Georgie.

Henry jerked back on the reins to bring his mount to a halt. He then leaped to the ground before the horse had even stopped moving, and he advanced toward his former friend with unbridled animosity.

"I ought to smash your nose into the back of your skull," growled Henry without preamble.

"Henry," said Wickham in obvious surprise. "Why have you come?"

"I thought you were my friend, but you intended to do *this* to me?"

"I am uncertain of your meaning, Henry."

"You know exactly what I am talking about, Wickham," said Henry, gritting his teeth. "You wrote that letter to Georgie. You know what she means to me, but you intended to run off with her and ruin her."

Wickham seemed to realize that it would be useless to prevaricate. "I *intended* to marry her."

"I am not a fool. I know you merely wanted to take her dowry for your own and avenge yourself against my brother. You have never held any tender feelings toward her. Georgie is much too innocent to interest a man of your proclivities. That is why I had never been concerned before. I had not realized I was housing a future turncoat under my roof."

"The girl is handsome enough," said Wickham. "She would make any man a good wife. You could give her to me, you know. She and I would not even have to elope—if you and I announced an engagement between your sister and me, she would not forsake it."

"Even before you attempted this stunt, I would not have entrusted my sister to a renegade such as you. I have seen you cheat at cards and frequent bawdy houses and taverns with the manic glee of one of the devil's own. I would never give my sister over to someone so utterly lacking in morals."

"You were by my side much of that time, Henry—"

"The difference between you and me, Wickham," said Henry grimly, "is that there is a line I will refuse to cross. I will never allow any harm to come to my sister."

Wickham gazed coolly at him, his eyes glittering in the moonlight. "If you are opposed to such a union, then I suppose I can leave her alone due to the years between you and me. Perhaps I can have my fun with one of the Bennet sisters."

"You will leave the Bennets alone, and you will leave these grounds."

"Why do you care what I do with the Bennets?" asked Wickham, throwing his hands in the air. "You would not give two farthings to keep your fiancée. I rather think you would pay someone to be rid of her entirely if you could only find the energy to exert yourself to do so."

Henry brought his voice low, a dangerous growl to it. "You will not touch any of the Bennets, least of all Jane. I may never have wished for her to be my bride, but I refuse to let her be sullied by the likes of you."

"Let me play my games with her, Henry. You can free yourself of her—"

"Leave her *alone*!" cried Henry.

Wickham continued as if Henry were not there, his voice taking on a pensive tone. "I suppose Jane Bennet has a greater share of beauty than most, even Georgiana. But Georgiana's *body*—"

Henry launched himself at Wickham, his arms clutching at the other man's throat. Both tumbled to the ground.

They rolled around on the grass, hitting and kicking and elbowing each other. Henry landed a punch on Wickham's face, busting his lip open.

After taking a moment to wipe off the upwelling blood, Wickham rallied and pushed Henry off him. He then landed atop him and swiped at Henry's face.

Henry caught Wickham's fist. "Surrender, ruffian. You know I have always been stronger than you."

"That may be so," said Wickham as he broke Henry's hold, "but I have always been craftier than you."

Henry opened his mouth to reply, only to shout due to a sudden flare of pain in his gut. With a Herculean effort, he shoved Wickham off him, cursing his name. He yanked the knife out of his abdomen and muffled his cry as he tossed it away from them.

"I should never have expected a fair fight from such a villain," groaned he, mostly to himself.

"It certainly was a mistake," said Wickham as he rolled toward Henry and engaged him once more.

A few minutes later, their faces and knuckles were both bloodied, and the grass and dirt had sullied their clothes beyond redemption.

They would have made even more of a mess of themselves had they not suddenly been ripped apart by Darcy, who kicked at Wickham to keep him away.

"A fistfight, Henry?" asked Darcy with a raised brow.

"There was a lesson that needed to be taught," said Henry with a shrug. He sat upon the ground, clutching at his wound and breathing heavily.

Frowning, Darcy fetched the lantern he had set aside and took a closer look at his brother. "Henry, what happened?"

Henry made a vague gesture. "Wickham's knife."

Darcy looked sharply at Wickham. "What cowardice was this, using a knife on an unarmed man?"

Wickham hobbled to his feet and moved closer, his posture stiff. He opened his mouth to say something biting, only to pale at the sight of the blood staining Henry's shirt.

Henry himself had pushed aside his unbuttoned coat to stare at the red overtaking the once-pristine whiteness, and he said inanely: "Quite a lot of blood."

"If my brother dies, Wickham," said Darcy in a dangerously low voice, "then I shall see to it that you meet an unhappy fate such as you have never imagined."

Wickham glanced from one Darcy to the other before he darted over to his horse. As Darcy shouted at him, he mounted the horse, which lunged as Wickham's heels dug into its side.

"You can chase after him, you know," said Henry, watching Wickham flee. "It would be unpleasant if he went unpunished."

Darcy shook his head. "Do not be a fool, Henry. We have to tend to you."

"Tend to me?" replied Henry before looking at his wound once more. "I suppose it does not appear particularly pleasant, does it?"

"You are slipping into delirium," said Darcy, removing his brother's coat. "Can you assist in pressing this against your wound? I need to lift you atop my horse."

"Certainly, certainly. Atop I shall go."

Elizabeth scarcely dared to blink as she stared out the drawing-room window for any sign of the Darcys' return. Her heartbeat drummed steadily in her chest as she waited, every minute that passed seeming like an hour.

Finally, Elizabeth saw the bouncing light of an approaching lantern, and she raised the alarm. "Someone is returning!"

Mr. Bingley exhaled heavily and then spoke. "I would request that everyone remain here. I will let you know if anyone's assistance is needed."

As Elizabeth watched him leave, she nearly followed him despite his request. Her sisters had been as anxious as she was since learning of what had happened, and Georgiana had been in such a wretched state that Mrs. Annesley had forced her to return to her chambers to rest. Lady Catherine had been filling any silence with rants about the foolishness of her nephews and an emphasis on how she had always believed George Wickham to be the utmost of scoundrels.

"Do you think anyone was harmed, Lizzy?" asked Jane in a quiet voice. Her wan face seemed filled with worry and fear.

"I do not know," said Elizabeth, "but I wish they had never left the house."

When the housekeeper finally entered the drawing-room, everyone looked to her for answers. She took in a deep breath and spoke in a voice that trembled. "Mr. Henry Darcy w-was wounded by Mr. Wickham. He is now in h-his room with his b-brother, and Mr. Bingley has left to bring the apothecary."

"May I assist while we wait for the apothecary?" asked Elizabeth anxiously.

Mrs. Williamson slowly nodded. "Yes. We will need cloths and water and bandages."

"Jane and I can help as well," said Kitty, looking to her eldest sister. Jane nodded in agreement.

"Yes, certainly, ah, please follow me then," said Mrs. Williamson. The poor old woman seemed heavily affected by what had happened, which would no doubt hamper her attempts at providing aid.

The three Bennet sisters worked to gather the materials needed at the frazzled directions of the housekeeper, and then they entered the room where Mr. Henry Darcy lay abed. His brother pressed a thick cloth onto his side, attempting to staunch any blood flow.

Henry Darcy had the pale appearance of a man who was having a brush with death, and Mr. Darcy seemed utterly distraught as he stared down at his brother.

"Please let us help, Mr. Darcy," said Elizabeth quietly. "You may sit down."

The gentleman nodded, and after Elizabeth directed Jane on taking over for him, he stepped away. Fumbling, he found his way into a chair nearby.

Though Elizabeth issued the initial directions on how to provide some small measure of relief and aid to Henry Darcy, Kitty quickly took over with a sort of single-minded insistence. Elizabeth felt surprised to see this from her sister, but she followed Kitty's instructions concerning such tasks as helping wrap the wound or placing a dampened cloth on the man's forehead.

"You are doing well," said Lady Catherine from behind them. Elizabeth turned in surprise, not having realized the woman had entered. The rare piece of praise seemed to be an indication of the mental state of her ladyship, which was probably no better than anyone else's in the house at present.

After ensuring his brother had been situated as best as he could while they waited for the apothecary, Mr. Darcy excused himself.

Seeing her opportunity to speak with him, Elizabeth quickly stepped out. Once she had closed the door behind her, she called out: "Mr. Darcy?"

The man turned and looked at her. "Yes, Miss Bennet?"

"Would you be able to spare a few minutes to advise as to what happened?"

Mr. Darcy's face darkened, no doubt due to his recall of what had transpired, but he nodded. "My brother reached Wickham before I did. When I found them, Wickham had stabbed Henry, and the two were rolling in the dirt like a pair of furious schoolboys."

Elizabeth grimaced. "Do you believe Mr. Wickham meant to kill your brother?"

"He may have simply been driven to use any method to win due to his cowardice. Regardless, I will ensure the authorities locate him and make him pay for what he has done."

Despite the circumstances, Elizabeth smiled at the protectiveness she heard in his voice. "Those under your protection must feel blessed. You are a very solicitous brother."

"I am afraid I must disagree with you, Miss Bennet," said Mr. Darcy firmly, shaking his head. "Had it not been for you, I would feel myself to be even more of a failure as a brother than I already do. I do not understand how Georgiana could have even considered doing something so foolish as eloping with Wickham."

"I fear you must try to think less about your feelings and more about your sister's in this situation, Mr. Darcy," said Elizabeth. "Georgiana is a shy girl, unaccustomed to attention from anyone but her family and her companion. It must have been easy for her to feel flattered by Mr. Wickham's words. Your sister is young and not to be blamed. You are not to be blamed either. Only Mr. Wickham should bear the blame."

Despite her words, Mr. Darcy did not meet her eyes. Instead, he appeared to be entrenched in such misery that Elizabeth's heart went out to him. She reached out and touched his arm with a careful gentleness. "*Mr. Darcy*."

The man's dark eyes settled upon her, filled with unmistakable anguish, and then he suddenly reached out and embraced her.

Elizabeth felt as if all the air left her chest at that moment. Both the surprise of the sudden gesture and the warmth of Mr. Darcy's body threatened to overwhelm her. But then her mind took over her senses, and she realized this man desperately needed comforting. With marked tentativeness, she reached up and lightly returned the embrace.

Into her hair, Mr. Darcy murmured: "I cannot thank you enough for the assistance you have provided to my sister—and, indeed, to my entire family. I know you must feel unkindly toward my family on account of my brother's behavior. Your goodness and your patience with Georgiana have made me feel astounded."

"Oh, Mr. Darcy," said Elizabeth quietly in response, "I do not feel unkindly at all toward your family. I must own that I did dislike your brother at one time, but when I witnessed his willingness to protect his sister, it made me realize there is a heart within Henry Darcy that I had failed to notice. I only hope that his heart will one day open toward *my* sister."

Mr. Darcy made an unintelligible noise against the crown of her head, and then he suddenly stiffened. He pulled away with a slight jerk. "I apologize, Miss Bennet. I—I forgot myself. Though I am distraught by what has happened, that is no excuse—"

"Actually, Mr. Darcy," said Elizabeth, interrupting him with a teasing smile, "I did not mind it at all. It felt quite pleasing to be able to comfort you, as if I might possess a sort of power over you."

"You do have a power over me, Miss Bennet," said he, his voice soft and barely audible.

Elizabeth's breath caught in her throat, and she wondered whether he intended to say more.

Rather than elaborate any further, however, he glanced away from her and said: "It is late, Miss Bennet. I think perhaps you may wish to retire to bed.

"As for me, I intend to reprimand Mr. Montgomery for his role with regard to Wickham's letter to my sister and attempt to determine whether he is a threat to the household or just a well-meaning fool."

"I do not intend to retire yet," said Elizabeth, "but I will rest once the apothecary arrives. Until then, I wish to assist my sisters and your aunt as best as I can."

"Thank you, Miss Bennet," said Mr. Darcy softly. She only smiled at him and returned to his brother's room.

CHAPTER XVII

Once the apothecary arrived, Elizabeth allowed herself to retreat to bed, her mind numb and her body weary from the onslaught of recent events. She fell asleep quickly, and when she woke at last to the sound of birdsong, she could not call herself well-rested, but she felt capable enough to face the rest of Haskett Hall's inhabitants.

Despite a preference for sleeping late, Kitty was absent from the room, so Elizabeth hurried to ready herself for the day with some brief assistance from the maid.

When Elizabeth walked into Henry Darcy's room, she saw Jane sitting beside the man's bed as Kitty worked to wring out a towel in a basin of water.

"You need not smother me with attention," growled Henry Darcy, reminding Elizabeth of a grumpy old dog being disturbed from its rest.

"We are not smothering you," said Kitty calmly as she placed the towel upon his forehead.

"The apothecary said you need not watch me every minute of the day."

"We do not wish to upset you, Mr. Darcy," said Jane in a quiet voice, "but the apothecary did tell us that we needed to be wary of any signs of fever."

"If anything happens, I can ring for one of the servants," said Henry Darcy.

"I think you would feel much better if you would take one of the draughts left by the apothecary," said Jane.

Looking at her older sister's hands, Elizabeth saw a slight fidgeting that betrayed Jane's worry.

"You may not realize it, Jane," said Kitty, "but this gentleman is incapable of listening to reason at present. I would suggest that you let me handle him."

"Bah!" said the gentleman referenced, crossing his arms with the air of a petulant child.

Kitty stared down sternly at him. "People who are wounded should be tended to."

"I have never needed a woman's care," said Mr. Henry Darcy, "and I do not need it now."

"It has been my impression that you have never truly understood what you need," said Kitty. "As such, you will have to abide being tended to by *women* until the arrival of the doctor."

Kitty met the man's glare with an unrepentant smirk.

Surprised by Kitty's interactions with the young man, Elizabeth glanced at Jane. But the other young woman simply stared at Kitty with a mild frown furrowing her brow.

A few minutes later, Georgiana Darcy rushed into the room.

"Henry!" cried she. "My aunt just told me that you were wounded by Mr. Wickham and that Mr. Montgomery has fled the house. Neither she nor Fitzwilliam will tell me what exactly happened, but I know it must all be my fault. I am so sorry, Henry!"

The girl then dissolved into tears beside her brother's bed, her head bowed into the bedding.

A surprised Kitty stood behind Georgiana, and Elizabeth saw Henry Darcy giving Kitty a helpless look, as if pleading for assistance with comforting his sister.

A moment later, Kitty stepped closer to Georgiana and put an arm around her shoulder. "Dearest Georgiana, you need not worry. Your brother is too stubborn to be overcome by a simple brawl, and Haskett Hall is better off without having someone of Mr. Montgomery's ilk within it."

"She has the truth of it," said Henry Darcy, his face having softened from the surliness demonstrated earlier. "I shall be fine, and we do not need Montgomery and Wickham's kind here."

"It is precisely as he has said, Georgiana," said Kitty. "Your brother is strong and will not be taken down easily by a villain such as Mr. Wickham. Instead of feeling regretful, we should all rejoice that Mr. Wickham's true character has been revealed to us. We know now not to welcome such a scoundrel among us."

"Your words are kind," said Georgiana, tears still running down her face, "but I know it must all be my fault. Henry would never have run after Wickham had it not been for me."

"It is not your fault in the slightest," said Elizabeth firmly, coming to the other side of the bed to gaze at Georgiana.

"We are all of the same belief," said Kitty, gently tugging at Georgiana so that she would turn and enable Kitty to look at her. Kitty then gave the girl a tender smile. "You know your brother will only feel worse if he thinks you blame yourself for what happened to him. You should remove any such notions from your mind."

Henry Darcy smiled gratefully at Kitty, and Georgiana sniffled a few times before she finally gave a vigorous nod. Kitty embraced her and murmured a few words of comfort before releasing her.

"Now," said Henry Darcy, "might you provide your dearest brother with a smile?"

The smile provided was tentative and weak, but it was given nonetheless.

"Now I can recognize my dear sister," said he warmly. But though Georgiana may not have noticed it, there was a stiffness to the man—or perhaps a tightness to his expression—that seemed to bespeak of the great pain that afflicted him. Still, the fact that he wanted to show his sister only cheerfulness could not help but further thaw Elizabeth's iciness toward him.

"I wonder whether I might request a few minutes alone with my nephew," said a voice near the doorway.

Elizabeth turned to look at Lady Catherine. Her ladyship appeared stern as she stared at the young man, and he grimaced at the sight of her.

"We will gladly allow the two of you some time alone," said Jane, speaking before anyone else had recovered from the surprise of Lady Catherine's sudden appearance.

Jane led the way from the room, and her sisters and Georgiana followed her. However, whereas Jane and Georgiana continued moving to stand further down the hallway after the door was closed, Elizabeth and Kitty exchanged a look and then pressed their ears against the wood, straining to hear the conversation within.

"Henry," came the sharp voice of Lady Catherine, "your behavior has been most wretched and unbecoming of your great lineage. If Sir Lewis were still alive to see what has become of you, he would give you a flaying the likes of which you have never seen before."

"I do not give two pins for my lineage," replied Henry Darcy, "and the threat of being whipped has never caused me to shirk."

Her ladyship remained quiet for a few moments, and Elizabeth thought she heard the woman give a huff. "Well, you shall listen to what I have to say regardless.

"You may have already received physical punishment for your foolishness, but you must endure a tongue lashing as well. I would never have dreamed that one of my relatives would act in such a reckless and callous manner, showing such a complete disregard for others."

"You are shocked. I can only understand that, as I had not exactly expected to find myself in this state either. Now, is there anything else?"

Lady Catherine's pause was much longer this time, and when she spoke, Elizabeth had to strain to hear her. "I know you have not realized it, but Jane Bennet is a lovely soul who deserves only the best in life. That she would have been required to marry such a rabid brute as you is the greatest of misfortunes.

"But even if you do not care about her, I know you care about your sister. You should think about how Georgiana deserves a brother who behaves in a much more becoming fashion than you do. One day, she shall be married, and when that day comes, do you want her to be embarrassed when you show your face to her new family? You should consider what will happen in the future in addition to what is happening in the moment."

In a voice that indicated a failure of patience, her nephew replied: "Will that be all?"

"I would scold you further if I thought it would have any effect," said Lady Catherine. "As it is, I intend to ensure that Miss Bennet knows my home will always be open to her once she has been shackled to you in marriage."

Hearing the finality in her ladyship's tone, Elizabeth and Kitty hastily backed away from the door and hurried over to stand near Jane.

Georgiana had apparently decided not to linger, as she was nowhere in sight.

Lady Catherine threw open the door and stepped out into the hallway, her irritation evident in the tightness of her face and the stiffness of her gait. She came and stood beside the three Bennet daughters, and then she looked to Jane. "Follow me, Miss Bennet."

Elizabeth and Kitty moved well out of the way to allow Lady Catherine and Jane to pass them. Once they had disappeared, Kitty murmured: "What do you think Lady Catherine wishes to say to Jane?"

"I suspect Lady Catherine intends to emphasize the fact that Jane will always be welcome in her home, as she mentioned to Mr. Henry Darcy," said Elizabeth quietly. "It is a benevolent offer, to be sure, but it is one that Jane shall never accept."

"I suppose I cannot disagree," said Kitty, "but I do not believe Henry Darcy is as callous as his bluster may make him seem."

"That may be," said Elizabeth, "but he is poorly suited to Jane, and I fear they shall never find happiness."

Kitty hummed in agreement, and then she and Elizabeth both returned to tend to the wounded Henry Darcy.

When the doctor arrived, his examination yielded a sort of cautious optimism. He emphasized that while Henry Darcy's condition appeared to be stable, that seeming stability could be overturned in a moment, and it necessitated that strict instructions be left for the young man's care.

Henry Darcy remained a surly patient, and Elizabeth felt her patience tested time and time again as he rebuffed well-meaning attempts to see to his comfort and health. However, Kitty remained tireless and unyielding, and Jane remained unperturbed by his irascibility. Only Elizabeth seemed to be especially exasperated by his behavior.

The most unusual aspect of the situation was Kitty's assumption of the mantle of the young man's primary caretaker. When his recovery faltered due to the onset of a high fever, Kitty remained with him through the night, dabbing at his forehead and murmuring comforting words whenever he descended into a delirium.

His improvement became more noticeable once he overcame the fever, and he began to clamor for release from bed rest, but Kitty met his short temper with her own and caused him to concede to her demands. The following day, Henry Darcy seemed quieter and contemplative, which Elizabeth attributed to being a result of the decrease of pain.

She was staring pensively at the young man as she sat near his bedside when his brother entered the room. Smiling, Mr. Darcy suggested that she join him on a walk.

"Please do, Miss Elizabeth," said Mr. Henry Darcy, attempting to infuse a bite in his words. "I will enjoy having a respite from the smothering presence of one of the Bennets."

Elizabeth merely rolled her eyes and indicated her eagerness to breathe in some fresh air.

She and Mr. Darcy had strolled some yards away from the house when she finally broke the companionable silence.

"I have been wondering at the change in your brother's mood," said she. "His reluctance to be coddled now seems to be something one might attribute to habit rather than desire."

"I have made a similar observation," said Mr. Darcy, "and I intend to broach the subject with my brother when I am able to conjure the appropriate words in my mind."

Elizabeth smiled and nodded. She knew it must not be easy for the brothers to engage in an earnest conversation given their differing temperaments, and she admired Mr. Darcy's willingness to put in the effort.

Hesitantly, Mr. Darcy asked: "Might I inquire as to how my sister has been handling the present circumstances? I know she finds me intimidating and does not always confide in me as I wish she would. She has attempted to reassure me that she is well, but there is a weakness in her words that causes me concern."

"I will own that she has not been quite herself, and she worries frequently that she is to blame for Mr. Henry Darcy's present condition. Still, your brother has been putting on quite the show whenever Georgiana is nearby, and I suspect it has helped her feel better, even if she is not entirely fooled by his act.

"Regardless, the fact that the worst of it seems to have passed will go a long way in soothing Georgiana's upset. Of course, it has done nothing for your brother's irritation, as my sisters will not let him leave his bed yet."

"Indeed," said Mr. Darcy with a nod. "I would, however, note that under normal circumstances, Henry would have left his bed behind him by now and would never have heeded his caretakers' warnings. I suspect part of that can be attributed to Miss Kitty's influence. I have noticed that she is apt to be stern with Henry about his health. As my brother is more accustomed to receiving such sternness from his relatives than his acquaintances, I do not believe he knows how to react, so his words are not as sharp and unkind as they might otherwise have been."

Elizabeth chuckled. "Your assessment seems sound. He is not the only one changing, however. My youngest sister, Lydia, has been a poor influence on Kitty during the past few years. Even though Kitty is two years older, she has always been inclined to follow Lydia around. Now that they have been separated, I believe Kitty has started to learn more about herself and what she wants from her life."

"I suspect part of that is the increase of your influence upon her," said Mr. Darcy.

Elizabeth shook her head. "No, I dare not attribute that much to myself."

"You should, for you can yield a great deal of influence over others without even realizing it."

Frowning, Elizabeth turned her head to look at him while they walked. "I suppose I do not quite catch your meaning."

But rather than elaborate, Mr. Darcy merely shook his head and smiled.

Some moments later, Elizabeth decided to change the subject. In the midst of the excitement surrounding Henry Darcy's wound, it had been easy to forget the reason he had been injured, but that reason had begun to weigh more heavily on her mind, and she resolved to address it with Mr. Darcy.

"I am worried about what might happen if Mr. Wickham comes back," said she suddenly.

"That was part of the reason I wished to speak with you," said Mr. Darcy, his voice grave but firm. "I received news this morning that the authorities have apprehended him."

Elizabeth felt a wave of relief wash over her. "I am glad to hear that."

"As was I. Fortunately, Wickham's actions toward Henry, coupled with the stack of gambling debts that have accumulated, will ensure that he cannot harm either of our families any longer."

Elizabeth closed her eyes to let the news soak in, the relief she felt almost palpable. Upon opening her eyes, she considered asking what Mr. Wickham's punishment would be, but then she decided it did not signify. She cared only that he would not be able to harm anyone else.

"Thank you for letting me know, Mr. Darcy."

"He is a greedy man," said Mr. Darcy, "but he is also spineless. I do not think he would have tried anything further, but I believed it to be best to take precautions regardless."

"I thank you for that," said Elizabeth, smiling at him. Upon witnessing the smile that he gave her in return, she found her heart warmed. She supposed that even considering everything that had happened, she could not ever regret meeting the Darcys.

That night, Darcy requested to speak alone with his brother for a few minutes. He wasted no time in coming to the point and said directly: "I have noticed a change in your attitude of late."

"I am not certain what you mean," said Henry.

"You seem a little calmer, a little less caustic. I merely wished to address the reason for such with you."

Henry sighed. "I suppose it would be too much to ask to forego this conversation."

"It would indeed."

"Very well," said Henry, looking down at his hands. "I suppose I *have* changed to an extent. My brush with death has made me reconsider how I have been living my life. You might say I am thinking about mending my ways."

"Hearing that brings me no small measure of relief. I have been concerned about you for a long time, Henry, and I suspect Georgiana has been as well."

Henry's gaze shot up to meet Darcy's. "Georgie? What do you mean, Fitz?"

Darcy looked at his brother for a few moments, studying the worry there. After the death of the elder Mr. Darcy, Henry had eschewed most responsibilities and cares, save for any that might pertain directly to Georgiana. But neither Henry nor Darcy had known how to raise their sister, so she had spent more time in the company of her companion than of either of them. Still, she had given Darcy glimpses of her worries on a few occasions, and now he began to wonder if Henry had not even seen that from her.

"While Georgiana rarely has an extended conversation with me," said Darcy, "she once expressed her belief that you would benefit from marriage to a suitable partner."

"Marriage? Did you tell her about my engagement to Jane Bennet?"

"I did not," said Darcy, "but she must have her suspicions about it. The fact that she never asked me why Jane Bennet and two of her sisters are staying at your estate makes me believe she must know."

Henry made an unintelligible noise and began to pick at a piece of imaginary lint, lost in thought.

Darcy stared at him for a long moment before he finally released a hefty sigh. "Henry, I think you need to break off the engagement."

Henry's surprise could not be mistaken. "Break off the engagement? Why would you make such a suggestion? You know our father wanted this connection to be made between us to assist the Bennet family. He requested it on his *deathbed*, Fitz. I always knew you to be prideful. Are you merely sneering at their social status—"

"This has nothing to do with the Bennets' social status," interrupted Darcy. "This is about Jane Bennet, that poor girl who has been tied to you through no fault of her own. She deserves someone better than you, Henry. She deserves someone who will treat her well—someone she *loves* or at least someone who will grow to love her."

"I never thought you to be the sort to subscribe to something so intangible as love, Fitz."

Darcy continued as if his brother had not spoken. "I know that Miss Bennet is not the type to complain about her lot in life, but she has to have been wounded by your obvious disinterest. What woman would not have been hurt by such treatment? Rendering assistance to her family through marriage will mean little if she ends up emotionally scarred by her relationship with her husband."

"Do you not care about what our father wanted?"

"What our father ultimately wanted was to help the Bennets," said Darcy. "Making Jane Bennet miserable will not accomplish that."

Henry opened his mouth as if to issue a rebuttal, but then he closed it and looked thoughtful.

"Consider what I have told you," said Darcy. "There are times when one must follow the heart of a request rather than the letter. The decision is ultimately yours, of course, but I do not believe that any good feelings between you and Miss Bennet can be salvaged."

Henry did not reply; instead, he remained quiet and contemplative.

CHAPTER XVIII

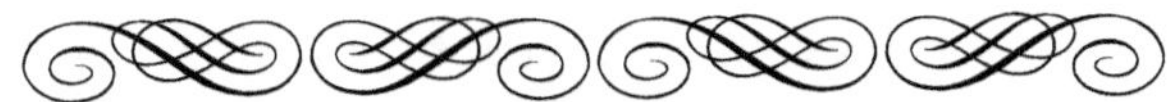

The next day, Elizabeth went to Henry Darcy's room to determine whether she needed to provide any assistance with his convalescence. Before she entered, however, she paused and peered inside. While the door had been left ajar, only Kitty could be seen within the room at the young man's side. Perhaps it was not strictly proper for them to be alone without the door fully open, yet Elizabeth supposed it could be excused due to the circumstances.

As Elizabeth watched Kitty interact with Henry Darcy, however, she found a frown creeping upon her face. There was a certain flirtatiousness to be seen in the way they were laughing together and meeting each other's eyes, and she wondered when the dynamic between them had changed. Just as surprising to her was the fact that there was something in the gentleness of the young man's smile that contained more substance than his usual smirk.

Elizabeth's frown deepened as she pushed the door fully open, and she crossed her arms as she stood there and stared at them.

"Ah, Miss Elizabeth," said Henry Darcy suddenly, having espied her, "I have good news that I wish to share. My caretakers have deemed me to be sufficiently recovered to sit at meals tomorrow."

"That is indeed good news if it is true," said Elizabeth, looking at her sister for confirmation.

Kitty smiled and nodded. "It is. He saw the apothecary not long before you entered, and he has been advised that if he continues using the draughts provided, then he is allowed to walk around in a limited capacity. His wound has been healing well enough that he shall be on his feet terrorizing the household before long."

Elizabeth refrained from retorting that he terrorized the household even without the benefit of moving freely within it. Instead, she said lightly: "I suppose his progress might be attributed to the gentle ministrations of his caretakers."

To Elizabeth's surprise, Henry Darcy smiled broadly and said: "It can indeed."

Staring at the young man, Elizabeth began to wonder if he had been replaced with a new person entirely.

A few days later, Elizabeth awoke to the jarring sensation of having her arm urgently shaken. She opened her eyes and blinked a few times, trying to focus on Jane, who hovered over her. Her sister's wan expression immediately drove away Elizabeth's grogginess.

"Jane, what is it?" asked Elizabeth, sitting up. "Has something happened to your fiancé?"

"These were given to me by a servant this morning," murmured Jane, lifting two letters that she had been clutching to herself.

Elizabeth tentatively raised a hand, and she took the letter that Jane held out first. Inhaling deeply, she began to read.

"DEAR MISS BENNET,

"I suppose a woman of your sensibilities must find yourself most scandalized by having received a letter from me when we scarcely say more than five words to one another if it can be avoided, but I believe you will find it in your heart to forgive me for the presumption, particularly since I have a much more important apology to proffer you.

"I wish to terminate our engagement forthwith.

"It should come as no shock to you that I bear you no affection, and since our engagement has been kept as a secret maintained by our family and close friends, I believe on the whole you shall not be harmed by my actions. Certainly, you can bear no love for me after the coldness I have displayed toward you.

"While I have never been much for sentimentality, I have been swept up by the violence of my feelings, and I may proclaim without any irony that I am in love with Kitty.

"I know you must scarcely believe me capable of any tender feelings, but I have come to recognize the importance of having someone at your side who is steady and true but also capable of bringing you laughter. My relationships with others have tended to be shallow, but after nearly dying, I understand the benefit of making every moment count.

"So that I may not waste any further time, I confessed my feelings to Kitty and suggested an elopement. She agreed, as we both believed that proclaiming our intention to her family in the hopes of having a normal wedding would only lead to the entire venture being forbidden. Thus it is that we have left for Gretna Green.

"I believe that our marriage shall be of benefit to all of us, as my marriage to your sister will still aid your family in the future should it be needed. Though it is not truly your place to do so, I would request that you please extend my apologies to my brother and sister.

"To the extent that they are required, you also have my sincerest apologies.

"HENRY DARCY"

Elizabeth had to review the piece of correspondence a second time to ensure she had not imagined what she read. Setting aside the fact that it was the worst apology she had ever seen put to paper, she could scarcely believe that Kitty would have agreed to such an outrageous plan. While she would never have called Kitty sensible, she would also have never expected her to run off in the night with a gentleman of such a short acquaintance in order to marry him.

Her shock must have been evident on her face when she looked at Jane, but her sister only handed her the second letter without speaking.

"MY DEAR JANE,

"I understand Henry has already explained everything in his letter to you, so I will not explain further. If by chance you have attempted to read my letter first, I would suggest you set mine aside and turn to his.

"I completely understand if you feel upset with me, and while I apologize for the rashness of my decision to leave with Henry, I do not apologize for breaking off your engagement with him. I never believed you loved him, and I know he did not care for you. The two of you would have made such a terrible match. La! He rarely even looked your way when you were nearby.

"I hope you are not angry with me. I worry the most about that. I do not believe it will signify much to my mother, and I know my father will merely shake his head and call me a silly, stupid girl.

"I do want you and Lizzy to know that we did take this decision seriously. Because we believed our families would not be supportive of our marriage, we decided to take matters into our own hands. Please forgive us both. I hope you

are not hurt, and I hope you are willing to call Henry your brother when you next meet.

"Yours, etc.

"KITTY BENNET"

Elizabeth did not need a second reading of this letter, for she felt in many ways it was simply an echo of Henry Darcy's. Both he and Kitty were emotional and foolish, and she supposed they would suit one another well, even if Haskett Hall would never profit without the extensive aid of Mr. Darcy and the estate's new steward.

After staring down blankly at the letter for a moment, Elizabeth gathered her wits about her and looked up at Jane.

Her sister's face remained without expression as their eyes met, and her mouth remained closed.

Tentatively, Elizabeth asked: "Are you hurt by what has happened, Jane?"

Jane shook her head slowly.

Elizabeth studied her sister's face for a long moment, trying to read her feelings without any success. "Are you upset about what might happen to your reputation, Jane? Or perhaps Kitty's or the Darcys'?"

Jane finally crumbled, bursting into tears. "Oh, Lizzy, I am so relieved!"

And then she embraced Elizabeth. Though startled at the sudden movement, Elizabeth, who remained seated in bed, patted her sister's lower back in comfort.

"I fear it makes me a terrible person," said Jane, "but I am so relieved that I will not marry Henry Darcy. I did not love him, and I should not be surprised if he disdained me. I know he has never respected me due to his resentment toward the situation in which we found ourselves. We would never have been happy together, and oh, I am so relieved!"

Jane descended into tears, and Elizabeth stood from the bed and clutched her tightly. "Oh, Jane—"

"Am I a bad daughter for having no desire to do my duty as I should, for—"

"Do not be silly, Jane!" cried Elizabeth. "Anyone with eyes could see that you and Henry were poorly suited for each other. While the suddenness of this development may come as a shock to us all, I believe that Henry Darcy and Kitty have grown to care for each other. Their relationship may not be steady, but some assistance from their families should smooth over any difficulties."

Jane swiped at her eyes with her fingers, nodding, and Elizabeth hastened to fetch her a handkerchief. After handing the item to her, Elizabeth said: "Now, I need to tell Mr. Darcy what happened. If you believe you are capable of the effort, I suggest that you write an express letter to Longbourn explaining everything."

Jane dabbed at her eyes with her handkerchief and said in a shaky voice: "I will do so."

After embracing her one more time, Elizabeth hastened to dress and then sought out Mr. Darcy.

Fortunately, he had risen early, and she located him in the study, speaking with the gentleman hired to act as Henry Darcy's new steward.

"Pardon me, Mr. Darcy," said Elizabeth, "but might I have a word alone with you on a matter of some urgency?"

Mr. Darcy nodded, and a few moments later, the steward had vacated the room.

"What has happened, Miss Bennet?" asked Mr. Darcy. "You appear to be distraught."

Elizabeth had not thought herself so easy to read, but she spared no further thought for that. "To explain the circumstances simply, your brother has eloped with Kitty."

A moment of silence passed, and then Mr. Darcy spoke. "I beg your pardon?"

"Your brother left with Kitty for Gretna Green, and they shall be married ere long. Mr. Henry Darcy sends his apologies to you and Georgiana."

Mr. Darcy stepped forward. "I will fetch my horse and try to stop them—"

"You need not charge ahead, Mr. Darcy," said Elizabeth, putting a hand on his arm before he could exit the room. "I doubt you would catch them even if you tried. Furthermore, while these circumstances are not ones that you or I would have chosen, I believe this may work out for the better. Kitty might be capable of issuing some measure of control over your brother in a way that Jane would not. In addition, they have indicated they feel great affection for one another."

Mr. Darcy hesitated, looking toward the door and then back to her. "Miss Bennet—"

"I believe the scandal will not be discussed for long," said Elizabeth. "Since the engagement between your brother and Jane was not widely known, the primary issue we face is that of the elopement. It is not an insurmountable problem."

Mr. Darcy nodded, his thoughts no doubt churning rapidly. "How is your sister—Miss Bennet?"

"Jane will be fine," said Elizabeth, smiling at the evidence of his concern. "I suppose my main concern is whether your brother truly will marry Kitty."

"He will do so," said Darcy, "or I shall run him through with a sword myself."

Though his words made her chuckle, Elizabeth could not help but think that Mr. Darcy had been half-serious.

A few hours later, Jane sat in the drawing-room alone. She had sent off an express letter to her father, as Elizabeth had suggested, and now she could afford herself the luxury of being lost in thought.

She felt a great deal of relief, but she also felt a great measure of guilt. As the eldest Bennet daughter, she bore the responsibility to do what she could to assist her family. For some time, she had believed the best way for her to do that was to marry Henry Darcy, thus securing the well-being of her sisters and mother upon the death of her father. Now, however, the weight of that burden had been lifted from her shoulders.

She might have felt even guiltier had it not been for Lady Catherine. Upon learning of the day's events, her ladyship had expressed brief aggravation toward her absent nephew. Minutes later, however, she had given Jane the barest hint of a smile and squeezed her shoulder. Jane had been warmed by the gesture, which she believed to be her ladyship's version of an embrace.

Now, Jane could relish the freedom of choice. She could allow herself to think of the future with a fragile hope rather than a heavy dread.

The sound of another entering the drawing-room caused her to lift her head. The sight of Mr. Bingley's approach made her pulse quicken.

"I heard what happened, Miss Bennet," said Mr. Bingley, looking upon her with concern. "Are you . . . Are you well?"

The worried look on his face, which was evident in the furrow of his brow and the tightness of his mouth and the crinkling of those kind—*always* kind—eyes, was nearly her undoing. She wished to destroy all her barriers and pour out her heart to him, expressing the depths of her relief and joy at her newfound freedom.

She did not do so, however. Instead, she exercised restraint and spoke to him carefully. "You need not be concerned for me,

Mr. Bingley, for my heart was not engaged. Rather, it was a marriage arranged by our families, and I am now released from it."

Mr. Bingley seemed surprised. "An arranged . . . arranged marriage?"

"Yes," said she, watching him. His worry was replaced first by relief and then by a growing happiness.

"I had not known," said he, smiling broadly and likely not even realizing it. "I had thought that perhaps . . . that perhaps you felt some measure of . . . well . . ."

"My feelings consisted only of obligation," said she. After hesitating a moment, she added, "But now I no longer feel even that."

Mr. Bingley's smile grew so wide his cheeks must have ached. "I am glad to hear that, Miss Bennet—so very, very glad. I wonder . . . once an *appropriate* amount of time passes . . . might you . . . that is . . . Could I court you the way you have always deserved to be courted? The way I have long desired to court you?"

Jane felt her jaw slacken in surprise. "Mr. Bingley?"

The man spoke in a rush, no doubt eager to say all he could before his courage failed him. "I have always admired you, Miss Bennet. You must have noticed my regard. I have feared the entire world could see it.

"Despite that, I knew I could not act upon anything due to your engagement, difficult though it was since I knew that you and Henry had never been a suitable match. I had feared that your engagement might have been the product of affection on your part. I am utterly relieved to hear that it was due to an agreement between families instead. I had hoped you would not find yourself in a loveless marriage, where you cared for your husband but received no affection in return.

"You might wonder at my words, Miss Bennet, but the truth is that I have fallen in love with you. I have seen the softness in your eyes as you try to look upon the world favorably, and I have witnessed your calm gentility. No other woman of my acquaintance would have handled Henry the way you have, without descending into anger and resentment. During these past months of our acquaintance, I have relished the quiet times we have spent together when Henry was out of sight and you briefly allowed yourself to be unguarded. I have known in my heart that the true Jane Bennet had been *that* dear girl who danced gracefully with me and spoke kindly to me when she did not feel the burdens of her engagement pressing upon her.

"My heart has been breaking for you, Miss Bennet. I desperately hope that you will let me court you and prove that I, unlike Henry Darcy, will be a dedicated and ardent suitor in my pursuit of your affections."

Mr. Bingley had never been especially skilled at keeping the emotions from his face, but now Jane could see them shining in full force. The hope that had been weak and fragile within her breast began to blossom, and Jane slowly smiled at him. "I think I would enjoy that very much."

Mr. Bingley beamed back at her in unbridled joy.

CHAPTER XIX

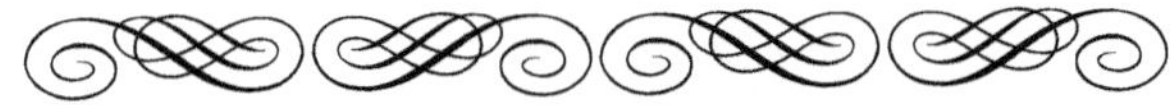

To the relief of those situated at Haskett Hall, Kitty and Henry did eventually return from Gretna Green as a married couple, deliriously happy, wildly in love, and not nearly as repentant as they should have been. In fact, Elizabeth would have gone so far as to call them utterly unabashed by their foolhardy actions. Even a thorough tongue-lashing from Mr. Darcy and Lady Catherine did nothing to sour Henry Darcy's mood, and Elizabeth and Jane's admonitions toward Kitty fell upon equally deaf ears.

Upon the return of the newlyweds, however, Mr. Bennet had deemed it to be prudent for Jane and Elizabeth to leave Haskett Hall, claiming that Kitty and Henry would need some time to themselves.

The return of Jane and Elizabeth to Longbourn was not welcome to Mr. Bingley, who did not wish to be parted from Jane, but he remedied the situation by leasing the estate of Netherfield, which had been available for some months. Mr. Darcy claimed that Mr. Bingley had needed to take up the lease and grow accustomed to estate management, but Elizabeth knew the truth of the matter, as her sister had shyly told Elizabeth about Mr. Bingley's confession about his feelings.

To Elizabeth's pleasant surprise, Mr. Darcy had followed Mr. Bingley to Hertfordshire, and so it was that a few months later found Elizabeth and Mr. Darcy walking upon one of Netherfield's many paths and trailing far behind a quietly conversing Jane and Mr. Bingley.

As Mr. Bingley laughed and leaned over to murmur something to Jane, Elizabeth felt her heart swell with gladness.

"They seem happy, do they not?" asked Elizabeth. Realizing belatedly she probably should not have spoken such words aloud, she looked at Mr. Darcy for his reaction.

He only smiled as he gazed upon the couple. "They certainly do. I had not realized how much Bingley's spirits had been dampened by my brother's coldness toward your sister. I suppose that is my failure as his friend."

"You could not have expected him to be eager to discuss your brother's fiancée with you."

Mr. Darcy chuckled. "No, I suppose I could not have."

Smiling, Elizabeth lifted her head and allowed her cheeks to be caressed by the sun for a few moments.

She felt as if the world had been set aright again. She did not even mind her mother's hints and proclamations about the two eldest Bennet daughters' marriage prospects, though the comments grew louder and more frequent by the day. Mrs. Bennet had been shocked at first upon hearing of Kitty's elopement, but she had been quick to rally and crow to any who would listen about the good match made by her daughter. Her triumph made her eager to look for further matches, and despite Elizabeth's attempts to quell her words, Mrs. Bennet made daily observations about Mr. Bingley's dedication to Jane and Mr. Darcy's to Elizabeth.

At the feeling of Mr. Darcy's eyes upon her, Elizabeth lowered her chin and glanced at him, slightly embarrassed at having tried to soak in the rays of the sun like a flower.

The gentleman tilted his head and gave her a warm look before returning his eyes to the path before them, his expression growing contemplative. "I hope you do not think too poorly of me on account of the way my brother bungled my family's relationship with yours."

"Oh, there is no need to apologize," said Elizabeth, "for no lasting harm has arisen from Henry and Kitty's trip to Gretna Green. The scandal was properly contained, and the elopement was entirely forgotten in the wake of the gossip that arose concerning the Earl of

Pembroke's marriage to a woman deemed so very far beneath him in status."

Mr. Darcy dipped his head, but the pensive expression did not leave his face, and his steps slowed such that they were soon quite far behind Mr. Bingley and Jane.

"I am glad you do not think ill of me," said he, finally slowing to a stop.

She ceased walking and faced him, tilting her head and wondering at the weight behind his dark gaze.

"In fact," continued he, his full focus upon her, "I hope that you might grow to think quite well of me in the future, Elizabeth."

Despite the closeness of their connection as in-laws, Elizabeth felt a flutter at his use of his given name. The feeling only exploded into a torrent of butterflies in her midsection at his next words.

"After all, I have fallen deeply and irrevocably in love with you."

"Mr. Darcy?" whispered she.

"I see you are stunned by my confession," said he, a wry smile on his face. "I had feared for a while that my feelings for you were too obvious. After all, your mother seems to have recognized them without any difficulty.

"But I have not been concerned about your mother's perception of us. Rather, I have worried that my brother's foolish behavior would reflect too poorly on me for you to look at me in any way but disgust."

Reading the nervousness in the gentleman's bearing, Elizabeth gave him a bright smile. "I suppose I need not remind you of my *sister's* foolishness. But I do wish to advise you that my feelings are quite the opposite of disgust. In fact, I feel that you have shown the depth of your character in the concern you have demonstrated for me and Jane and Kitty and even the other foolish members of my family. Many would find themselves frightened away by my mother's forwardness."

"Elizabeth," said he, the word seeming to catch in his throat as he took a step closer to her, "dare I presume that your feelings might not be wholly unlike my own?"

She tilted her head and gave him a coy smile. "I suppose you might say that my feelings closely mirror yours."

"Do you—that is—"

Pitying him, Elizabeth extended her heart toward him: "I love you, too, Mr. Darcy."

The relief seemed to spread throughout his entire body as the tenseness left his shoulders and his worried expression melted into one of happiness. "Elizabeth, would you please do me the honor of becoming my wife?"

Her smile so broad that her cheeks felt the strain, Elizabeth said: "Yes, Mr. Darcy, I will marry you."

Mr. Darcy came toward her, extending his arms, and she entered them without hesitation. He pressed her tightly to him, kissing the top of her head through her bonnet, and then he gently withdrew a few inches from her and slowly lowered his mouth to meet hers.

Elizabeth had time to pull away if she desired, but she felt no such inclination; instead, she lifted her face and met his lips with her own.

The kiss fell somewhere between the gentleness of a sigh and the warmth of a promise, and though Elizabeth wished to extend it, she knew should not indulge herself on this occasion. So it was that she slowly pulled back, her eyes lifting to meet Mr. Darcy's darkened gaze.

"I apologize for my forwardness, Elizabeth," murmured Mr. Darcy, who did not sound apologetic at all.

"Though I know I should deny it and demure, I must own that I appreciated your forwardness."

He laughed. "Demureness was not a quality that drew me to you, as you should well know, but I dare say my happiness concerning your acceptance was of such a great magnitude that it could not be contained."

"My happiness was no less than yours," said she warmly, "and I anticipate a lifetime of happiness before us, with the occasional quarrel to drive away any danger of monotony."

"No life with you could ever be monotonous, Elizabeth."

She tilted her head and stared up at him with a raised brow. "I must warn you that I have been acquainted with wildly outspoken women who became as meek as sheep upon marriage."

Mr. Darcy shook his head, more out of amusement than disagreement. "I have faith that you shall always be true to yourself."

"Except when I feign to hold opinions that are not my own."

"Even that is a part of you, for your brightness of mind must lead you to turn the conversation into new and exciting directions."

"Perhaps," said Elizabeth with a vaguely mysterious air.

"But I dare say that is enough talk," said Mr. Darcy abruptly. "Now, we must seek your father's permission so that we may wed as soon as may be."

Elizabeth laughed at his eagerness. "I dare say we might first tell Jane and Mr. Bingley that we intend to part with them."

Mr. Darcy caught her hand and pressed a kiss upon it. "I shall never let go of you as long as I live, Elizabeth."

"I shall hold you to that."

"Please do, dearest Elizabeth. Please do."

CHAPTER XX

After parting ways with Jane and Mr. Bingley, Elizabeth and Mr. Darcy turned back to Longbourn, engaging in a brief discussion of the appropriate appellation for her to use to refer to him in private.

"Perhaps I should call you 'Fitz' as your brother does," said Elizabeth, giving a playful smile.

"I would much rather you did not."

Elizabeth laughed. "Very well. I suppose 'Fitzwilliam' is a name that would do as well as any."

"Indeed, I should much prefer it," said Fitzwilliam. Though his words were spoken in a solemn tone, a smile tugged at the corners of his mouth.

"I suppose I must do what I am able to please my fiancé."

"Your fiancé is much obliged for your attention to his wishes."

"Then you must also abide by *my* wishes," said Elizabeth, lifting her head and tilting it.

"And what would those wishes be?"

"That you continue to call me by my Christian name as often as you dare."

"I think I can manage that quite often, Elizabeth."

Elizabeth knew the slight thrill she received upon hearing her name spill from his lips would only be a temporary occurrence, but for now, she felt resolved to be madly and violently in love and to experience all the attendant pleasures and griefs. "Then I shall do the proper amount of pining whenever you are not at my side."

"I think I have already done quite enough of that for both of us."

Elizabeth laughed and grinned up at him with unbridled happiness. "It pleases me to hear it."

"That is well, as it embarrasses me to say it."

It was with this happy attitude that they passed through the entrance to Longbourn, where Fitzwilliam wasted no time in requesting an audience with Mr. Bennet.

Elizabeth asked Fitzwilliam if he wished for her to remain with him, knowing her father would not mind her presence. But Fitzwilliam shook his head and advised he could handle it on his own. Elizabeth covered her smile as she read the nervousness on Fitzwilliam's face as easily as she would a book, and she left him so that she could sit with her mother and sisters in the drawing-room.

"I must own that I am surprised by your request to speak with me, Mr. Darcy," said Mr. Bennet. "I had not been aware that there was any business to be discussed between us. Do you need to talk to me about Haskett Hall?"

"I do not," said Darcy, "though my purpose is multifold."

"Quite mysterious," said Mr. Bennet, studying his face. "I would never expect that from you, so my curiosity is especially piqued. What is the first order of business then?"

Darcy hesitated. Perhaps he ought to lead up to the most important item of the day, but he rather thought Mr. Bennet would appreciate directness. Furthermore, Darcy did not want to draw out his nervousness any longer than was necessary.

Resolved, Darcy said bluntly: "I would like to request Miss Elizabeth's hand in marriage."

Sitting behind his desk, Mr. Bennet blinked at Darcy in astonishment. "I beg your pardon?"

"I have asked Elizabeth to marry me, and she has agreed. We now only lack your blessing."

"Well," said Mr. Bennet, "well."

"Sir?" asked Darcy, his anxiety increasing at the other man's reaction.

"I suppose I am not especially surprised that you would have recognized the value of my Lizzy. After all, you have spent a lot of time in company together, and you have more sense than your brother has displayed. If you were any other man, I might feel obligated to tease you until the sweat drips from your brow, but I cannot deny a man such as you anything."

The relief that came over Darcy was nearly a tangible thing. "I am glad to hear it, sir. I had feared this conversation would be more trying. I think the world of Miss Elizabeth, but I had indeed suspected you might seize upon the opportunity to tease me."

"I find it wholly unnecessary to engage in such a thing in front of such an upstanding young man as yourself. I fear I must warn you, however, that Henry will likely remain my favorite son-in-law. He is much easier to tease, as his countenance is not nearly so foreboding."

Darcy grimaced at the reminder of his brother. "I also wanted to take the opportunity to apologize in full for my brother's actions. I know my brother did not act honorably in traveling to Gretna Green with your daughter."

Mr. Bennet waved a hand in the air. "You need not apologize. I had always expected either Kitty or Lydia would do such a thing sooner or later. I am only thankful Lydia did not abscond with one of the redcoats before they left Meryton. Our family's reputation can survive one elopement, but two such elopements might very well cause the value of our name, such as it is, to plummet."

"This situation between our families has been somewhat . . . unusual," said Darcy cautiously. "If you will not deem it to be too intrusive, I would like to ask why the marriage between my brother and your eldest daughter was arranged to begin with. My father had been disinclined to pass on the details, only issuing a strong request that the engagement be upheld."

Mr. Bennet sighed. "I suppose there is no harm in educating you about the past. However, the story is one I do not especially enjoy telling, in part because of the pain of your father's passing and in part because of my own embarrassment.

"Your father and I were friends at school. Longbourn turned a fair profit in those days since my father had more of a knack for business than I do, but when I eventually married a woman whose connections were unimpressive, the gap between me and your father only widened.

"Before that time, however, we were close acquaintances."

"Was this close acquaintance the reason my father wished for an alliance between our families?" asked Darcy.

Mr. Bennet shook his head. "Your father would not have been swayed for such a reason. No, the real reason can be attributed to the foolishness and passion of youth.

"As you are aware, your father's health suffered at times, but his pride never weakened because of it. When a fellow student—a nasty man by the name of Gates—insulted your father, your father began to issue a challenge. I naturally cut him off, knowing he would not survive a confrontation with Gates. I issued the challenge myself then, proclaiming that I would not stand by while my friend's honor was insulted. Gates scoffed at the situation, but I goaded him into accepting. I felt confident he could not best me."

Darcy grimaced but remained quiet, allowing Mr. Bennet to continue the story.

"We were to fight until one of us was unable to proceed, and I won the duel. Still, the experience left me severely injured, and my face suffered from the experience, as flesh does none-too-well when met with the blade of a sword.

"Your father was equal parts regretful and thankful as he sat by my bedside. Though I boasted that I was impervious to death, we both worried I might die. I told him that if I survived, then he could repay his debt by sending me one book a year."

"One book a year?" asked Darcy with an upraised brow.

"Yes, your father's reaction was not much different from that," said Mr. Bennet with a chuckle. "He scoffed and indicated he would one day determine a much more fitting way to repay me, and I merely dismissed his promise.

"My health eventually returned, though I was left with a limp and a scarred face. We grew further apart after we finished our education, and my passions led me to marry for love. Fortunately, my wife was not turned away by my scarred face, as many other young women were. Of course, it did not take long for me to realize that my wife had little sense to speak of, and my passions began to diminish. Over a period of years, I was then struck by the blows of a succession of five daughters, no heir, and no inclination toward business."

"When did you see my father again?" asked Darcy.

"Lydia was scarcely more than a toddler when your father showed up at Longbourn. He proclaimed he had been passing through Hertfordshire and felt desirous of seeing an old friend. With Mrs. Bennet's perpetual wails about the entail on Longbourn, you can imagine that it did not take long for your father to comprehend the situation that I faced. He and I met in my study in private, and he said we should arrange a marriage between his youngest son and one of my daughters."

Darcy frowned. "He did not speak with my mother about it first?"

"It is possible he came to Longbourn knowing more than I thought he did, but he may also have been guided by his passions. All I know for certain is that he believed the arrangement between our families would pay back his debt and assist my family. I tried repeatedly to convince him that the idea was a poor one, but I finally conceded."

"I never expected to hear such a tale as this," said Darcy.

"Young men are often guided by their passions, so it should not be surprising. You are not much different from your father—after all, you must be aware that my Lizzy has little dowry of which to speak."

"I have no need of a large dowry," said Darcy. "Rather, I desire a happy marriage."

"I know," said Mr. Bennet with a smile. "That is why I am willing to let Lizzy go. I desire no less than the best for her."

"I want the same," said Darcy firmly.

"Then I suppose all that remains to be settled on is a date," said Mr. Bennet. He waved a dismissive hand. "Now, please forgive me if I do not join you in the drawing-room. I would request that the announcement be made at once and that the door to my study remain closed. Mrs. Bennet's exultations will no doubt rival the shrieks of a plucked chicken, and I would rather not subject my ears to them."

Smiling, Darcy said: "I suppose I can do you such a favor."

Mr. Bennet laughed and waved for him to depart the room. "Out with you, then. And remember to firmly close the door."

After shutting the door behind him, Darcy shook his head in amusement and walked to the drawing-room. Once inside, he met Elizabeth's questioning look with a smile, and her relief at his buoyant mood was obvious.

"It is a pleasure to see you, Mr. Darcy," said Mrs. Bennet, looking between him and Elizabeth. "Would you not like to sit over here near Lizzy?"

"I rather believe she has an important announcement that must not be delayed."

Elizabeth's lip twitched—perhaps she had wanted to keep their engagement secret for a little while longer—but her mother's obvious interest meant the subject could no longer be put off. "Mama, I suppose you might be pleased to hear that Mr. Darcy and I are now engaged."

Mrs. Bennet did not immediately comprehend the news, but once she did, her eyes widened, and the crowing predicted by Mr. Bennet began in earnest. "Ah, I knew it! I knew you would be engaged soon! I knew all along that my dear Lizzy would make a match with such a fine young man! Your wit had to mean something to a man interested in that sort of thing!"

Mr. Bennet's description of his wife's shrieks seemed quite apt, and Elizabeth appeared to be aggrieved by her mother's loud words. But Darcy, though he would ordinarily find that such outbursts irritated him or at least made him uncomfortable, could only smile. His happiness could not be contained. He felt as if his world were finally complete.

Epilogue

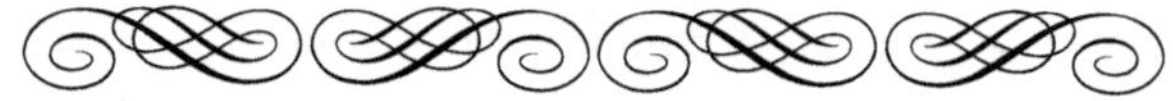

lizabeth dodged a pair of young boys running around the field and made her way to a little girl who sat crying in the grass.

Without hesitating, Elizabeth gathered her skirts and sat down beside the girl. She had to do so carefully, however, as she was with child, and the swell of her stomach had already begun to make maneuverability more difficult. "Little Janey, what happened?"

Her daughter sniffled and said in a breaking voice: "E-Edward and T-T-Thomas pushed me over, Mama."

Elizabeth placed a hand on her shoulder. "Oh, Janey. Though that was unkind of them, I do not believe they intended to harm you."

She glanced at Edward, who was the spitting image of Henry, and then at Thomas, who had Jane's nose but his father's eyes. She could not help but smile at the sight of them as they wielded long sticks as swords and swatted at one another with raucous calls.

Elizabeth, Jane, and Kitty had decided to spend the afternoon picnicking with their husbands and children. The area felt hectic—perhaps too hectic for Fitzwilliam's liking, though he would never have complained—but it brought joy to Elizabeth nonetheless.

Nearby, Kitty held a squirming baby while a toddler tugged at her skirts. Henry stood a few feet from her, smirking but also gazing at her with a love that had never seemed to diminish despite everyone's predictions to the contrary.

"Up, up," cried Bingley as he tossed a giggling two-year-old boy up into the air. He always doted on both his children without reserve.

"Be careful, Charles," admonished Jane gently as she watched, her hand coming to rest on her stomach. She, too, had found herself to be with child again.

Elizabeth embraced Janey and then encouraged her to get to her feet. Fitzwilliam stood before them in an instant to aid Elizabeth in standing, and she smiled at him in thanks.

Elizabeth supposed their gatherings would grow even larger in time. Though Mary remained unmarried, one of the Bennets' cousins seemed particularly interested in her piousness, and they might be engaged ere long. Lydia did not have any children at present, and she was traveling with her husband, a redcoat who was too much of a flirt for Elizabeth's liking. As for dear Georgiana, the girl was newly married, and while Fitzwilliam heartily disapproved of the man whom his sister had chosen, Elizabeth knew his mind would change in time. Georgiana's husband was quite likable, after all—friendly to a fault, much like Charles Bingley.

Janey suddenly threw herself at her father's legs, bursting into tears and explaining what had happened to her. Fitzwilliam picked her up and led her and Elizabeth to a nearby blanket which they soon sat upon.

"Boys are mean!" cried Janey.

Fitzwilliam's face remained serious as he listened to her complaints, and Elizabeth smiled at him. She felt blessed to have married a man who made such a wonderful husband and father.

As Fitzwilliam worked to comfort Janey, he slowly reached out and took Elizabeth's hand, giving it a soft squeeze.

She squeezed his hand back before she made a small gasp of surprise and touched her stomach.

Fitzwilliam and Janey both turned to look at her, and Janey immediately forgot her current woes to descend upon Elizabeth's stomach. Reaching a hand out and giving a gentle stroke, Janey asked: "Was it the baby, Mama?"

Elizabeth smiled. "Yes, Janey, it was."

"I cannot wait until I am a big sister!"

"I cannot wait either, dear one."

"I hope I have just as many sisters as you, Mama," said Janey. "I do not want any brothers!"

Elizabeth chuckled. "I am not certain my wishes are the same as yours, but I certainly would not mind a few more girls."

"As long as they are healthy," said Fitzwilliam, "I do not care if they are girls or boys."

Elizabeth smiled at him, and he smiled back at her. She would never have thought that the arranged marriage of one of her sisters would lead them all on such a journey, but she would not change what had happened for the world. Though children could be difficult to tend to at times, and marriage was never a completely smooth road, her heart was full and warm.

The End

PRIDE AND PREJUDICE VARIATIONS FROM ONE GOOD SONNET PUBLISHING

By Lelia Eye
A Sister's Sacrifice
Netherfield's Secret

By Colin Rowland
The Parson's Rescue
Hidden Desires

By Jann Rowland
Acting on Faith
A Life from the Ashes (Sequel to *Acting on Faith*)
Open Your Eyes
Implacable Resentment
An Unlikely Friendship
Bound by Love
Cassandra
Obsession
Shadows Over Longbourn
The Mistress of Longbourn
My Brother's Keeper
Coincidence
The Angel of Longbourn
Chaos Comes to Kent
In the Wilds of Derbyshire
The Companion
Out of Obscurity
What Comes Between Cousins
A Tale of Two Courtships
Murder at Netherfield
Whispers of the Heart
A Gift for Elizabeth
Mr. Bennet Takes Charge
The Impulse of the Moment
The Challenge of Entail
A Matchmaking Mother
Another Proposal
With Love's Light Wings
Flight to Gretna Green
Mrs. Bennet's Favorite Daughter
Her Indomitable Resolve
Love and Libertine

ALSO FROM ONE GOOD SONNET PUBLISHING: PRIDE AND PREJUDICE COLLABORATIONS

By Jann Rowland & Lelia Eye

WAITING FOR AN ECHO
Waiting for an Echo Volume One: Words in the Darkness
Waiting for an Echo Volume Two: Echoes at Dawn

A Summer in Brighton
A Bevy of Suitors
Love and Laughter: A Pride and Prejudice Short Stories Anthology

By Jann Rowland, Lelia Eye, and Colin Rowland

Mistletoe and Mischief: A Pride and Prejudice Christmas Anthology

PRIDE AND PREJUDICE SERIES FROM ONE GOOD SONNET PUBLISHING

By Jann Rowland

COURAGE ALWAYS RISES: THE BENNET SAGA
The Heir's Disgrace
*Volume II Untitled**
*Volume III Untitled**

NO CAUSE TO REPINE
A Tacit Engagement
*Scandalous Falsehoods**
*Upstart Pretensions**
*Quitting the Sphere**

* Forthcoming

Other Genres by One Good Sonnet Publishing

FANTASY

By Jann Rowland & Lelia Eye

EARTH AND SKY SERIES
On Wings of Air
On Lonely Paths
*On Tides of Fate**

FAIRYTALES

By Lelia Eye

The Princes and the Peas: A Tale of Robin Hood

SMOTHERED ROSE TRILOGY
Thorny
Unsoiled
Roseblood

* Forthcoming

About the Author

Lelia Eye has lived in Arkansas all her life. While she enjoys watching movies and reading, she refuses to subject herself to any books or movies with unhappy endings.

Lelia has been interested in writing since she won a short story contest in the sixth grade. Her imagination has been active far longer than that, as her childhood was filled with stories built around such villains as dogcatchers with unflappable determination and pirate ponies with hearts of gold.

Her interest in Jane Austen was sparked when she took a Jane Austen class in college. Her other writing interests include the realms of fairy tale, fantasy, and the supernatural.

She lives with her husband of more than ten years and two precious daughters as well as some geriatric fur-babies.

Website: http://onegoodsonnet.com/
Facebook: https://facebook.com/OneGoodSonnetPublishing/
Twitter: @OneGoodSonnet
Mailing List: http://eepurl.com/bol2p9

www.ingramcontent.com/pod-product-compliance
Lightning Source LLC
LaVergne TN
LVHW010947110826
845149LV00015B/3242

* 9 7 8 1 9 8 9 2 1 2 3 6 3 *